YU XUN, JIA GUO, AND YU CHENG

These are Cao Cao's chief advisors, who keep an eye on the royal court and advise of any potential threats or mutinies. They are the ones who alert Cao Cao to a possible revolt from within the royal court and caution him against embracing Bei Liu too closely.

BU LU

Bu Lu is known and feared as one of the greatest warriors in the world. However, during the battle of XiaPi, Bu Lu was overtaken by those he never thought to suspect: his own men. Now, having been handed over to Cao Cao, Bu Lu will do and say things that make his friends and his enemies question everything they know about him.

GONG CHEN

Gong Chen is an advisor who once served Cao Cao before defecting to serve Bu Lu. Like his master, Gong Chen was captured at the battle of XiaPi and brought to Cao Cao as a prisoner. Unlike his master, Gong Chen will behave in a way that testifies to a deep sense of courage and honor.

LIAO ZHANG

Liao Zhang is another of Bu Lu's subordinates who was captured at the battle of XiaPi. Utterly defiant of his captors, Liao Zhang is about to be put to death by Cao Cao when Yu Guan intervenes and pleads for his life to be spared. Yu Guan vouches personally for Liao Zhang's honor and worth, and Liao repays the debt by treating Yu Guan as his savior.

BEI LIU AND THE SWORN BROTHERS

Bei Liu, Yu Guan, and Fei Zhang are sworn brothers who have pledged their lives to the restoration of China. However, along the way they have been driven from one area to the next, and have been forced to make choices that compromise the nature of the oath they took to each other and the nation. Most recently, they have entered into an alliance with Cao Cao, a man they despise but whom they rely upon for survival. The alliance allows Bei Liu to be close to the royal court, particularly the emperor, who discovers that Bei Liu is his uncle by descent. When the emperor and Bei Liu become close, Cao Cao immediately suspects a mutiny is in the works. When Cao Cao humiliates the emperor during a royal hunting party, Yu Guan insists they deal with Cao Cao then and there. But Bei Liu insists on being patient, asking his brothers to lay low for a while. Bei Liu then joins into a blood pledge with several members of the royal court committed to defeating Cao Cao.

Some time later, Cao Cao invites Bei Liu for a drink. Bei Liu knows he is being interrogated by Cao Cao, but deflects his questions until they are interrupted by the news that Shu Yuan and Shao Yuan are about to form an alliance. Sensing a chance to ingratiate himself to Cao Cao, Bei Liu offers to attack Shu Yuan. Cao Cao gives him 50,000 soldiers and sends him out to do so.

While they are away, Bei Liu and his brothers receive word of Cao Cao's murderous rampage after he discovered evidence of the blood pledge. Bei Liu sees this horrific moment as the right one to finally attack Cao Cao, which is fortuitous, as Cao Cao is on his way to meet them with an army of 200,000 soldiers.

CHENG DONG

Cheng Dong is an elder of the royal court whose sister is one of the emperor's mistresses. Cheng Dong is also one of the masterminds behind the blood pledge to take down Cao Cao, and he convinces Bei Liu to join the cause. His actions must be carried out with the utmost caution and secrecy, because there are ears everywhere in this age.

EMPEROR XIAN

Emperor Xian is the supreme ruler of the Han Dynasty who is nonetheless controlled by Cao Cao. He reaches out secretly to several royal advisors, and eventually Bei Liu, asking them to pledge an oath to take down Cao Cao. But the plan goes awry when Cao Cao discovers who is assisting the emperor, and the resulting list of victims will extend well beyond those who wrote their names in blood.

SHAO YUAN

Shao Yuan is a temperamental leader who is as likely to attack someone for a petty grievance as he is to retreat in the face of a genuine threat. When he attacks Zan GongSun in the north, Cao Cao dispatches Bei Liu to defeat Shao Yuan's brother, who is seeking an alliance. Bei Liu then asks Shao Yuan to join him in the fight against Cao Cao, which could end up being one of Bei Liu's worst decisions.

FENG DIAN

Feng Dian is an advisor to Shao Yuan, who recommends his master to join Bei Liu's effort to defeat Cao Cao. However, not for the first time, Shao Yuan's fickle nature will confound and sadden those around him.

Chapter 1

The Fall of Bu Lu AD 198

Summary

Bu Lu is known and feared as one of the greatest military commanders in history. But he is betrayed by his own men during the battle for XiaPi. They bring him to Cao Cao, along with Liao Zhang and Gong Chen. Bu Lu asks to be spared and pledges to serve Cao Cao, but Bei Liu reminds him of Bu Lu's tendency to kill those he has sworn to serve. Bu Lu immediately and desperately begs for his life until he is admonished by Liao Zhang, who insists he stand up and face his fate like a man. Liao Zhang's life is spared by Cao Cao after Yu Guan personally vouches for his worth and virtue. Liao Zhang then pledges himself to Cao Cao's service. In stark contrast, Gong Chen refuses to listen to anything Cao Cao has to say, and goes to his death with his head held high.

After Bu Lu and Gong Chen have been put to death, Yu Guan goes to the cell where Diao Chan is imprisoned. He intends to kill her so that she won't be able to manipulate Cao Cao into killing Bei Liu, as an act of revenge for Bei Liu's role in Bu Lu's death. But Diao Chan has no interest in furthering the bloodshed, and Yu Guan doesn't have the heart to kill her, so he lets her go.

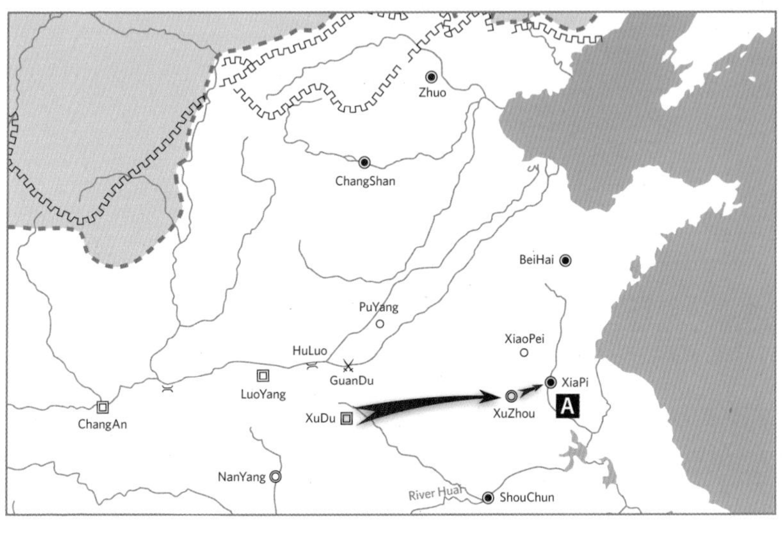

A After many battles over many years, Bu Lu is captured in XiaPi and put to death in 198 AD.

Unlikely Friends: Yu Guan and Liao Zhang

When Liao Zhang is brought before Cao Cao, he expects to be put to death like his master, Bu Lu. However, Yu Guan steps forward and asks for Liao Zhang's life to be spared. Yu Guan remembers the soldier from previous battles against Bu Lu, and remembers him to be both noble and loyal. Liao Zhang considers Yu Guan to be his savior, and is loyal to him even though he serves Cao Cao.

CRNCH CRNCH

LOOSEN THESE CHAINS!
THEY'RE DIGGING INTO ME!
CHNG

DEAL WITH IT. I'M NOT ABOUT TO LET A WILD TIGER OFF ITS LEASH.

CAO CAO, YOU'VE WON! YOU'VE BROKEN MY MIND AND BODY. YOU DON'T NEED TO TORMENT ME ANYMORE.

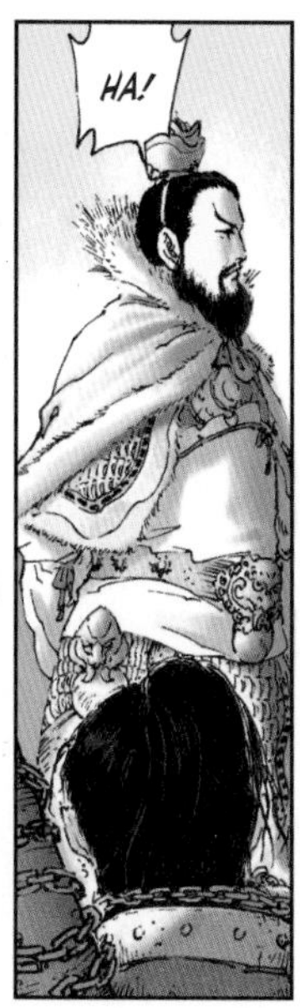
HA!

THOSE CHAINS ARE STRONG.
SO YOUR PHYSICAL DEFEAT IS APPARENT.

BUT I AM NO DEITY, SO I CAN'T SEE INTO YOUR MIND. HOW, THEN, WOULD I KNOW IF IT'S BROKEN OR NOT?

BY LISTENING TO ME! IF YOU SPARE MY LIFE, I WILL PLEDGE IT TO SERVING YOU.

HA HA HA!

DID I HEAR THAT RIGHT?
THE WORLD'S GREATEST KILLER WILL PLEDGE HIMSELF TO ME?
WHO NEEDS THE THRONE? I FEEL LIKE I'VE ALREADY WON THE WAR!

WHAT DO *YOU* THINK ABOUT BU LU'S PLEDGE OF LOYALTY, BEI LIU?

I THINK BU LU HAS A HABIT OF KILLING THOSE HE'S PLEDGED TO SERVE.

HA HA HA!

MIND YOUR TONGUE, YOU FILTHY LIAR! YOU WERE THE ONE WHO STOLE THE LAND FROM BENEATH OUR FEET AND THEN LIED IN ORDER TO DRIVE US OUT! WE DON'T OWE YOU ANYTHING!
HOOSH

IS THIS HOW YOU REPAY MY CHARITY?
SHUT UP, BEI LIU! I WILL KILL YOU FOR THAT!

YOU SEE, BU LU?
YOU'VE ALREADY OUTLIVED YOUR USE IN THIS WORLD.

THE WORLD MAY BE DONE WITH ME, CAO CAO, BUT YOU STILL HAVE USE FOR ME, DON'T YOU? I CAN LEAD YOUR ARMY TO VICTORY, AND YOU TO THE THRONE!

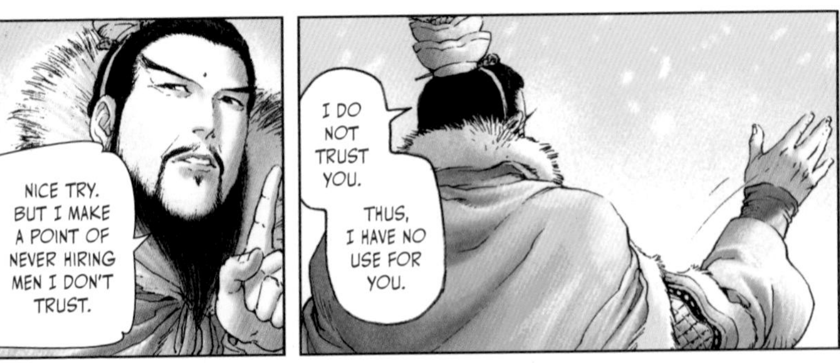
NICE TRY. BUT I MAKE A POINT OF NEVER HIRING MEN I DON'T TRUST.
I DO NOT TRUST YOU.
THUS, I HAVE NO USE FOR YOU.

CAO CAO, PLEASE! I AM BU LU! THERE IS NO LIMIT TO WHAT I CAN DO!

SPARE ME, AND I WILL DO WHATEVER YOU ASK.

IT'S TOO LATE, BU LU. YOU CAN'T FACE WEST AND HOPE TO SEE THE SUN RISE. HOLD ONTO YOUR PRIDE AND DIE A SOLDIER'S DEATH. WITH HONOR.
I DON'T HAVE TO BE A SOLDIER! I'LL LIVE LIKE A DOG IF I MUST. YOUR DOG!
I'LL FOLLOW YOUR EVERY ORDER. IF YOU TELL ME TO BARK, I'LL BARK. IF YOU TELL ME TO BITE, I WILL BITE.
HACH, SPIT
BU LU, YOU COWARD! STAND UP LIKE A MAN, NOW!
WE ALL HAVE TO DIE SOMEDAY! COME TO GRIPS WITH THAT!

DON'T YOU DARE SIT THERE WAILING LIKE A SWADDLED CHILD!
I SWORE MY LIFE TO A MAN WHO IS A DRAGON, NOT SOME SNIVELING TRAMP! DON'T MAKE ME REGRET THAT!
WHAT ABOUT ALL THE MEN WHO GAVE THEIR LIVES IN YOUR NAME? ARE YOU TRYING TO DISGRACE THEIR SPIRITS?

YOU ARE BU LU!
NEVER FOR-GET!

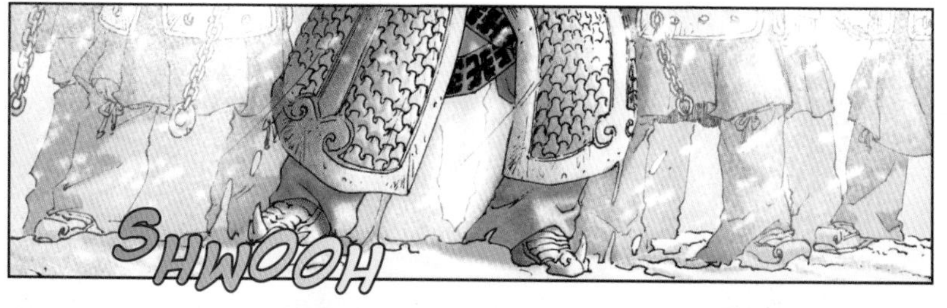
SHWOOH

HYOOOH

HWOOA

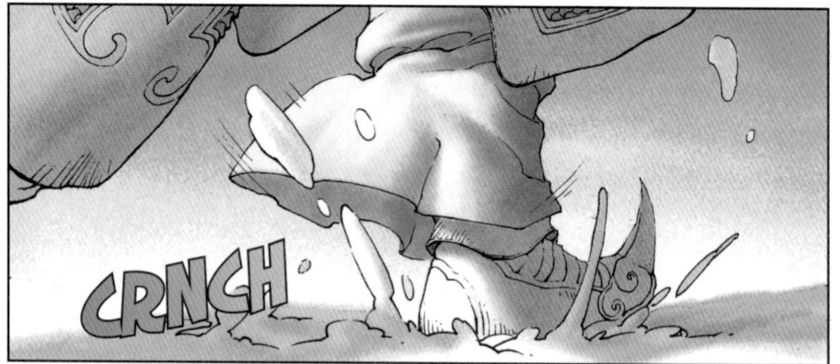
CRNCH

THE WORLD WILL NOT FORGET YOU, BU LU.
YOU WILL LIVE ON IN LEGEND FOREVER.

WHAT A SPEECH! BRAVO!
CLAP
CLAP

YOU ARE HANDLING THIS BETTER THAN HE IS. I RESPECT THAT.
YOU LOOK FAMILIAR. HAVE WE MET BEFORE?

YES, WE'VE MET BEFORE.
WE FACED EACH OTHER IN BATTLE WHILE PUYANG BURNED.
IT'S A SHAME, REALLY...
WHAT'S A SHAME?
IT'S A SHAME I DIDN'T THROW YOU INTO THE FLAMES WHEN I HAD THE CHANCE!
HOW DARE YOU SPEAK TO ME THAT WAY!
NOW I WILL PERSONALLY DISPATCH YOU TO HELL!
SHING

NO, MY LORD, WAIT!

IF I MAY...
HIS NAME IS LIAO ZHANG.

HE IS HEADSTRONG, AS YOU CAN SEE.
BUT DON'T BLAME HIM FOR BU LU'S ACTIONS.
LIAO ZHANG IS KNOWN TO MANY AS A GOOD AND RIGHTEOUS YOUNG MAN.

SPARE HIS LIFE.
I WILL VOUCH FOR HIM PERSONALLY.

HM.

WHOOSH
!
!
HM...

BLINK
SHUNK
I'VE SPENT HALF MY LIFE IN BATTLE, AND I'VE FACED DEATH MORE TIMES THAN I CAN COUNT.
I'VE ALSO CAUSED ENOUGH DEATH FOR TWO LIFETIMES.

BUT I DID NOT TAKE UP ARMS JUST TO KILL PEOPLE. I DID IT TO SAVE THE HAN DYNASTY, TO SPARE PEOPLE FROM SUFFERING.
IF YOU THINK THAT MAKES ME A MONSTER OR A TRAITOR, THEN TAKE MY SWORD AND KILL ME.
MY LORD!
WHAT ARE YOU-?
STAND BACK.

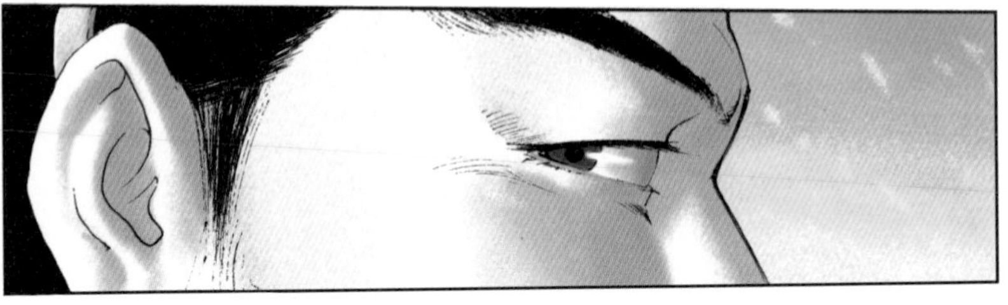

MY LORD...

WELL? GO ON. WHAT ARE YOU WAITING FOR?

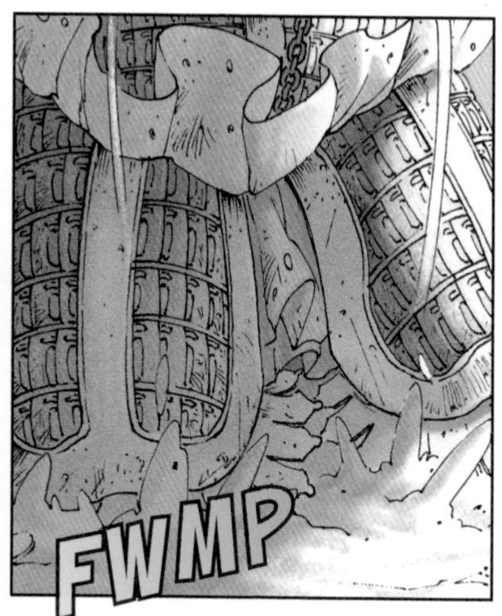
FWMP

FORGIVE ME, MY LORD, FOR NOT SEEING THE VIRTUE OF YOUR EFFORTS. IF YOU SPARE ME, YOU WILL HAVE MY THANKS AND MY PLEDGE TO SERVE YOU.

DON'T THANK ME, LIAO ZHANG. THANK YU GUAN. IF IT WEREN'T FOR HIM, YOU'D BE DEAD ALREADY.

EITHER WAY, I'M HAPPY YOU WERE ABLE TO MAKE UP YOUR OWN MIND ABOUT ME.

THERE IS MUCH TO DO, AND VERY FEW I CAN TRUST. I CAN USE MAN WITH SUCH STRENGTH OF CHARACTER.

YOU'RE GOOD AT USING PEOPLE.

AH, GONG CHEN! IT'S BEEN A WHILE, OLD FRIEND.
SPARE ME YOUR WORDS.
I HAVE NO TIME LEFT FOR GAMES.

AND TO THINK, YOU ONCE SAVED MY LIFE. FATE CAN BE CRUEL.

YES, IT CAN.
AND FOR SAVING YOU, I DESERVE TO DIE.
IF I HAD LET YOU DIE, THIS WOULD BE A DIFFERENT WORLD.

BEI LIU! WHAT HAVE YOU GOT TO SAY FOR YOURSELF?

THE GHOSTS OF XU PROVINCE WILL HAUNT YOU FOR JOINING FORCES WITH CAO CAO!

CALM DOWN, GONG CHEN.
YOU'RE TOO AMBITIOUS TO THINK YOU CAN TALK YOUR WAY OUT OF THIS.

AMBITIOUS?
I WILL NOT BE LECTURED ABOUT AMBITION BY A MAN WHO WANTS THE THRONE, AND WILL LIE, STEAL, AND KILL TO GET IT!
I AM NO THIEF, GONG CHEN.
AND MY *ONLY* AMBITION HAS BEEN TO SAVE MY PEOPLE AND MY COUNTRY.
MY CONSCIENCE IS CLEAR.

IS IT? THEN YOU'VE DECEIVED EVEN YOURSELF.
BUT YOU HAVEN'T DECEIVED THE GODS, NOR WILL YOU ESCAPE THEIR WRATH.
GODS?
WHAT GODS? LOOK AROUND YOU...

THE GODS DIED LONG AGO! THERE'S NOTHING LEFT BUT AN EMPTY HEAVEN!

I RECALL SOMETHING YOU SAID LONG AGO.
YOU SAID, IF WE DON'T GIVE UP ON THE WORLD, THE WORLD WON'T GIVE UP ON US. I SHOULD HAVE KNOWN IT WAS NOTHING MORE THAN THE PROVERB OF A POISONOUS SNAKE.

GONG CHEN...

YOU CLAIM TO LOVE THE WORLD, YES? THEN WHY RESIST WHEN THE WORLD CHANGES? WHY DON'T YOU ACCEPT THAT THE WORLD MUST NATURALLY REORDER ITSELF FROM TIME TO TIME?

YOU LOVE THE WORLD?
THEN LEARN TO BOW YOUR HEAD AND SWEAR TO UPHOLD THE NEW ORDER OF THINGS.

THERE IS NOTHING NATURAL ABOUT A WORLD THAT'S BEEN CHANGED BY WAR.
I HAVE SEEN THE NEW ORDER OF THINGS, AS YOU SAY. AND I WILL DIE WITH MY HEAD RAISED BEFORE I BOW TO SERVE THAT.
GONG CHEN!

SIGH
GO IN PEACE, THEN. YOU HAVE CHOSEN TO DIE WITH HONOR.
IN RETURN, I PLEDGE TO CARE FOR YOUR FAMILY. FOR OLD TIMES' SAKE.

THANK YOU, CAO CAO.
Once upon a time, Gong Chen and Cao Cao were allies. But time, war, ambition, cruelty, and malice had taken an irreparable toll on their friendship, and as Gong Chen marched to his death, the world fell into a cold, mournful silence.

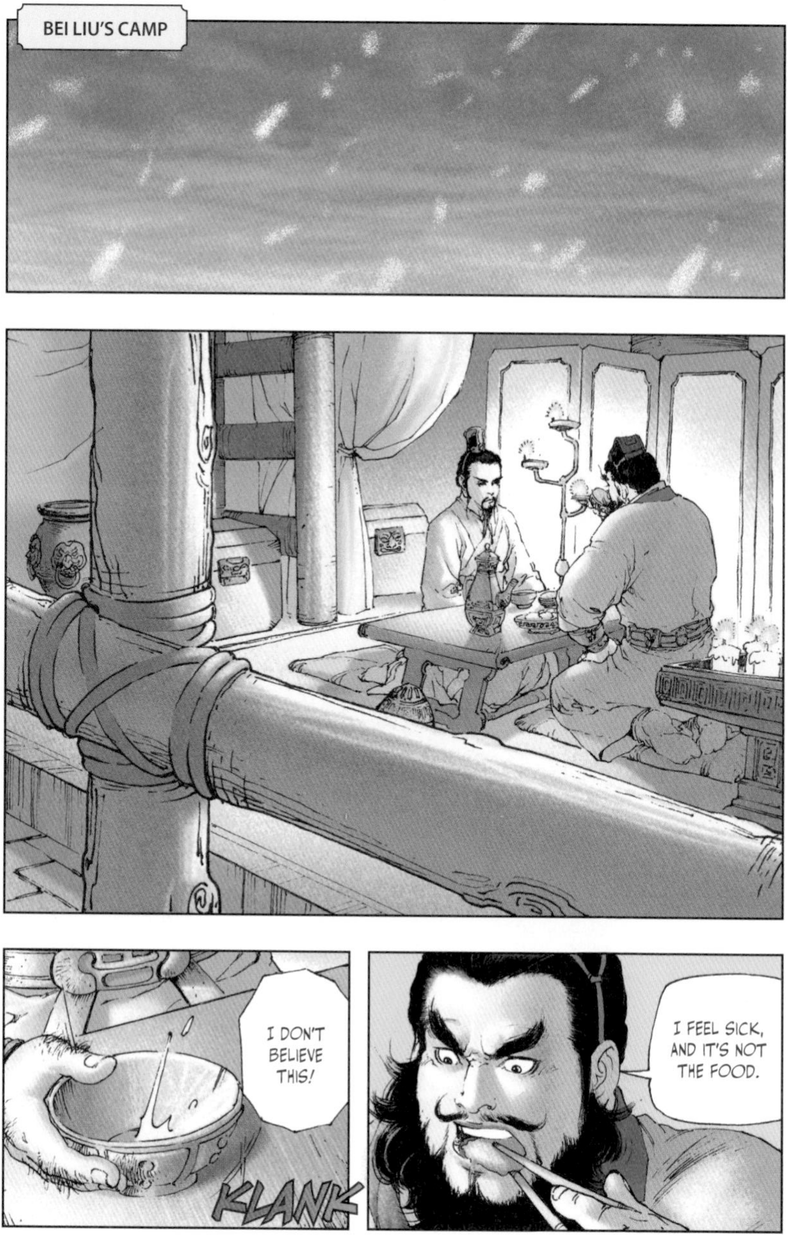

BEI LIU'S CAMP

I DON'T BELIEVE THIS!
KLANK

I FEEL SICK, AND IT'S NOT THE FOOD.

CAN YOU BELIEVE THE WAY BU LU ACTED TODAY?
IT TURNS MY STOMACH TO SEE A SOLDIER BEGGING FOR HIS LIFE LIKE THAT.

EVEN GONG CHEN HELD ON TO HIS DIGNITY. WHO WOULD HAVE THOUGHT HIM THE BETTER MAN?

MY LORDS, MAY I COME IN?

LIAO ZHANG!
OF COURSE, COME IN!

HAVE YOU SEEN COMMANDER YU GUAN?
I WISH TO SEE HIM.
I'M AFRAID HE'S NOT HERE AT THE MOMENT. WHY DON'T YOU HAVE A DRINK WITH US WHILE WE WAIT FOR HIM?
THANK YOU, BUT I REALLY SHOULDN'T IMPOSE.
YU GUAN SAVED MY LIFE OUT THERE TODAY.
I WISH TO THANK HIM PROPERLY.
I'LL COME BACK WHEN HE RETURNS.

HOW DO YOU LIKE THAT? NOT LONG AGO THEY WERE MORTAL ENEMIES. NOW HE OWES HIS LIFE TO YU GUAN. THIS WORLD IS SO CONFUSING.

≡ YAWN ≡
ALL RIGHT, I'M GOING TO SLEEP.

I CAN'T WAIT FOR YU GUAN ANY LONGER.

HE HARDLY EVER DRINKS WITH US. OH, WELL. HIS LOSS.
DOES HE HAVE A SECRET MISTRESS OR SOMETHING?
BRUUUP, EXCUSE ME...

MEANWHILE, IN A NEARBY JAIL

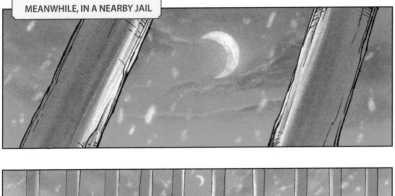

SNOW FALLS FROM A CLEAR SKY...

...AND THE EARTH IS SHROUDED IN A BLANKET OF WHITE.
EVEN THE STARS MOURN WHAT WE'VE BECOME.

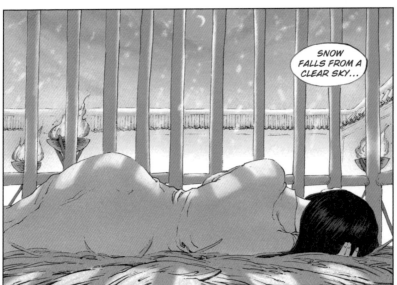

THERE IS SILENCE, BUT THERE IS NO PEACE.
THE WORLD IS DEAF TO MY PAIN...
...AND WANTS US BURIED DEEP AND FORGOTTEN.
I CAN'T HEAR YOUR FOOTSTEPS. I CAN'T HEAR YOUR HEARTBEAT.

IT IS SAID THERE IS A WOMAN IN THE NORTH...
...WHOSE BEAUTY IS UNSURPASSED.
KREEK

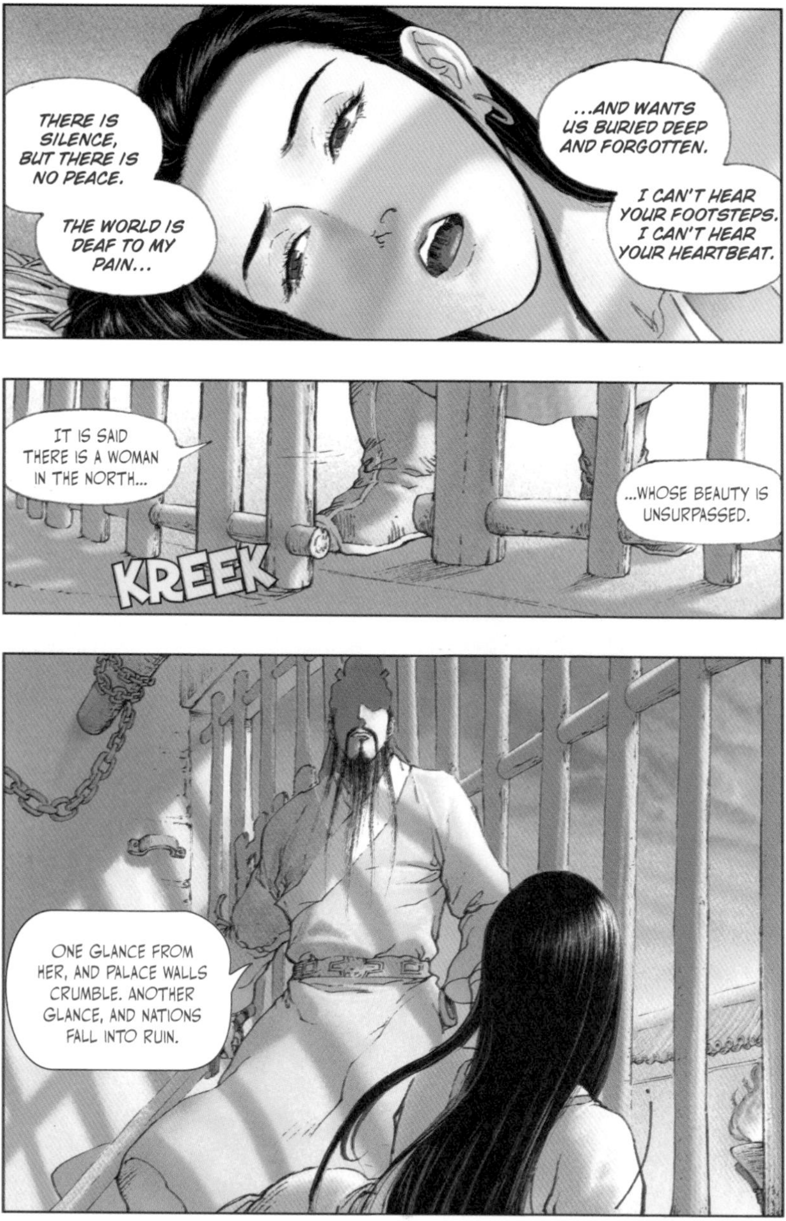

ONE GLANCE FROM HER, AND PALACE WALLS CRUMBLE. ANOTHER GLANCE, AND NATIONS FALL INTO RUIN.

AND YOUR DESIRE TO SHARE THIS WITH ME BROUGHT YOU HERE?
I KNOW WHAT YOU DID TO ZHUO DONG AND BU LU.
I CAN'T LET YOU DO IT TO CAO CAO.
SO LET ME SEE IF I UNDERSTAND YOU CORRECTLY. THEY WERE TWO OF THE MOST POWERFUL AND DANGEROUS MEN ALIVE. THEY COMMANDED ARMIES THE SIZE OF NATIONS AND BENT AN EMPEROR TO THEIR WILL...
AND I SOMEHOW DEFEATED THEM WITH A GLANCE? THAT DOESN'T SPEAK VERY HIGHLY OF THEM.

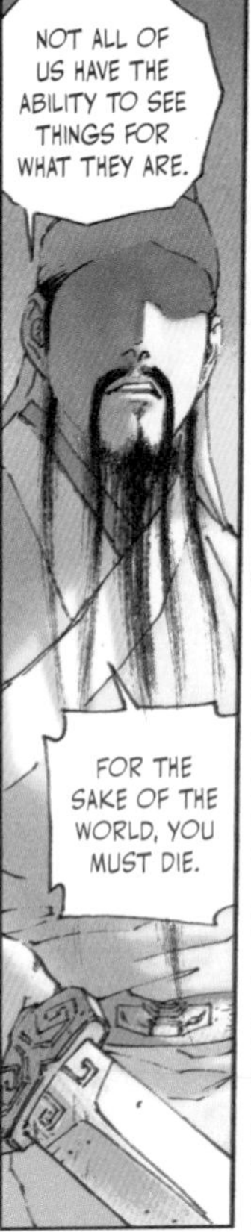
NOT ALL OF US HAVE THE ABILITY TO SEE THINGS FOR WHAT THEY ARE.
FOR THE SAKE OF THE WORLD, YOU MUST DIE.

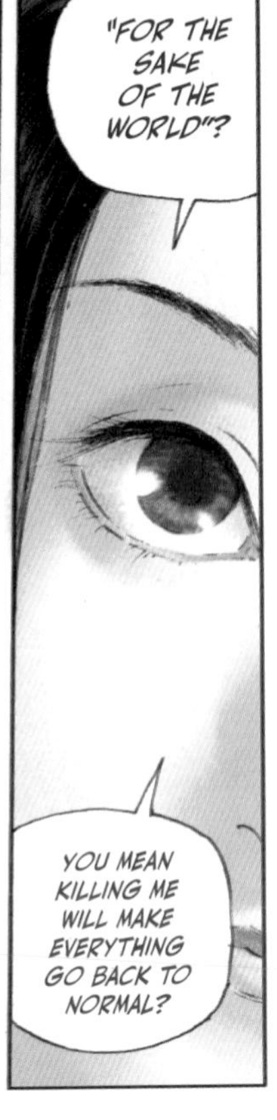
"FOR THE SAKE OF THE WORLD"?
YOU MEAN KILLING ME WILL MAKE EVERYTHING GO BACK TO NORMAL?

ENOUGH WITH THE GAMES! THERE'S TOO MUCH AT STAKE.
AND THAT'S WHY YOU MUST SHED THIS WOMAN'S BLOOD WITH YOUR NOBLE BLADE?
THAT'S RIGHT. THE FATE OF THE WORLD DEPENDS ON IT.
DON'T BE ABSURD. IN YOUR MIND, BEI LIU IS THE WHOLE WORLD. YOU'RE AFRAID I'M GOING TO SET CAO CAO AGAINST HIM TO AVENGE BU LU'S DEATH.

BUT I'M THROUGH WITH ALL THIS. FINISH ME, IF YOU MUST. I'M TIRED OF OUTLIVING THOSE I LOVE.

!

KRANG
LEAVE THIS PLACE. AND FORGET IT EVER EXISTED.

Chapter 2

Bei Liu and the Blood Pledge AD 199

Summary

After Bu Lu's execution, the emperor invites the royal court to the palace for a celebration. There he learns that Bei Liu is his uncle by descent. Upon this discovery, the emperor asks Bei Liu to save his life by getting rid of Cao Cao. Meanwhile, Cao Cao's advisors alert him to the threat of a revolt; it turns out the celebration was part of an elaborate scheme for Cao Cao to be able to identify who his enemies might be. Cao Cao then decides to draw out those enemies by calling for a hunting party. During the hunt, Cao Cao embarrasses the emperor, which infuriates Bei Liu and his brothers. But, rather than wage open revolt, Bei Liu asks his brothers to leave the city and lay low for a while. Bei Liu then signs a blood pledge with several members of the royal court, an oath to overthrow Cao Cao and save the emperor. The other members want to attack Cao Cao immediately, but Bei Liu suggests patience, insisting that the right time will come.

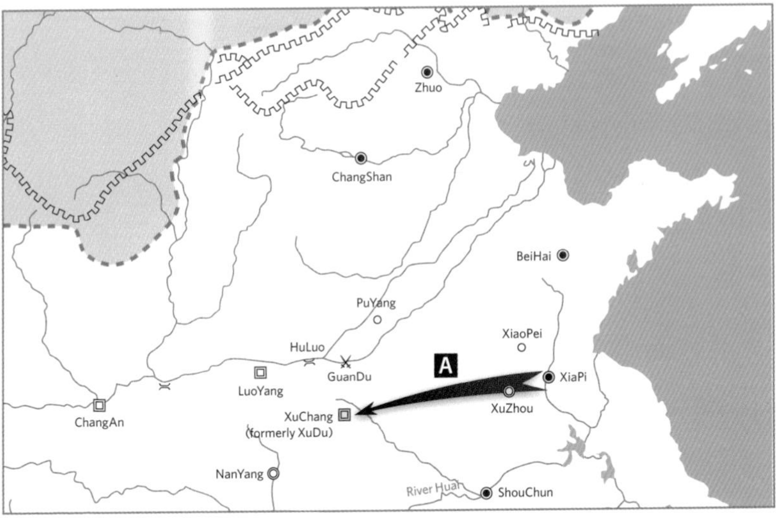

A After defeating Bu Lu, Cao Cao and Bei Liu return to XuChang (formerly XuDu; Cao Cao changed the name to "Chang," which means prosperity) and attend a royal celebration at the emperor's palace.

The Emperor's Secret Order

Emperor Xian suffers greatly at the hands of Cao Cao, who controls all matters of the state, both civil and military. Empress Shou Fu advises the emperor to seek the help of Cheng Dong, so the emperor composes a royal order, written in his own blood, that reads, "Remove Cao Cao." He then hides the order in his robe and secretly delivers it to Cheng Dong. The order, and the pledge written in response to it, will be eventually be discovered by Cao Cao, with deadly consequences for those who the emperor asked for help.

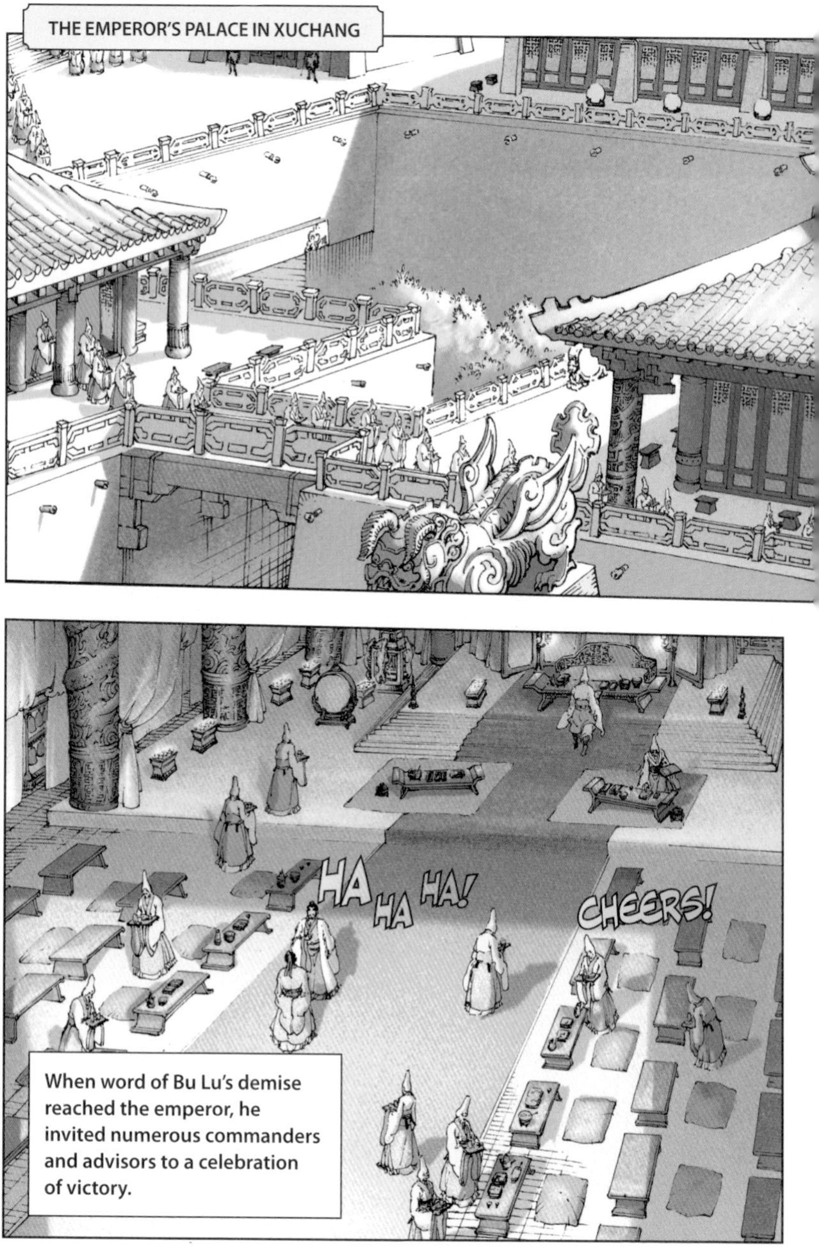

THE EMPEROR'S PALACE IN XUCHANG

HA HA HA!

CHEERS!

When word of Bu Lu's demise reached the emperor, he invited numerous commanders and advisors to a celebration of victory.

RONG KONG! SO GOOD TO SEE YOU AGAIN.
CHENG DONG! HOW HAVE YOU BEEN?

I TRUST BEIHAI IS UNDER YOUR PEACEFUL CONTROL?
CHENG DONG
PEACE-FUL? HA!
THERE'S NO SUCH THING THESE DAYS.

COME, SIT HERE.

DO YOU KNOW WHY CAO CAO HAS SUMMONED YOU TODAY?

THAT'S EASY...

RONG KONG
HIS TREACHEROUS LITTLE SCHEME IS PRETTY OBVIOUS, ISN'T IT?
HE'S TRYING TO FIGURE OUT WHO HIS ENEMIES ARE.

SH! BRIDLE THAT TONGUE, BEFORE IT GETS YOU KILLED!

INDEED, DISASTER THREATENS TO STRIKE ANYONE WHO DARES TO PREVENT THE HAN DYNASTY FROM FALLING! *HA HA HA!*

SO, RONG KONG...

WHAT'S CAO CAO UP TO THESE DAYS?
YOU TELL ME.
YOU'RE A MEMBER OF HIS ROYAL COURT.

CAO CAO DOESN'T TELL US ANYTHING.
WE KNOW HE'S UP TO SOMETHING, BUT WE'RE POWERLESS.

HOW ARE THINGS ON THE OUTSIDE?

SHU YUAN WAS BROUGHT TO RUIN.
BU LU IS DEAD.
NOW WE'RE ALL WAITING TO SEE WHAT BEI LIU DOES.
BEI LIU?
HE'S CAO CAO'S ALLY, ISN'T HE?

HE HAS DONE MANY THINGS TO RESTORE HIS REPUTATION.
EVEN THE PEOPLE OF XU DON'T HAVE A BAD WORD TO SAY ABOUT HIM.
THINGS HAVE CHANGED, MY FRIEND. THAT WAS SOME TIME AGO.
HE'S A DIFFERENT MANNOW.

INDEED.
IT'S CLEAR CAO CAO VALUES HIM GREATLY.
THAT'S WHY BEI LIU HAS SUCH A HIGH RANK.
WELL, LET'S NOT GET AHEAD OF OURSELVES.

I'VE HEARD. SURELY HE MUST HAVE HIS OWN AMBITIONS, BUT CAN WE TRUST AN ALLY OF CAO CAO?

REMEMBER, THOUGH, THAT EVERYTHING WITH CAO CAO IS A PLOT OF SOME KIND.
HE'S USING BEI LIU'S POPULARITY TO MAKE PEOPLE FORGET THAT HE CONTROLS THE EMPEROR.

ATTENTION, EVERYONE! ATTENTION!

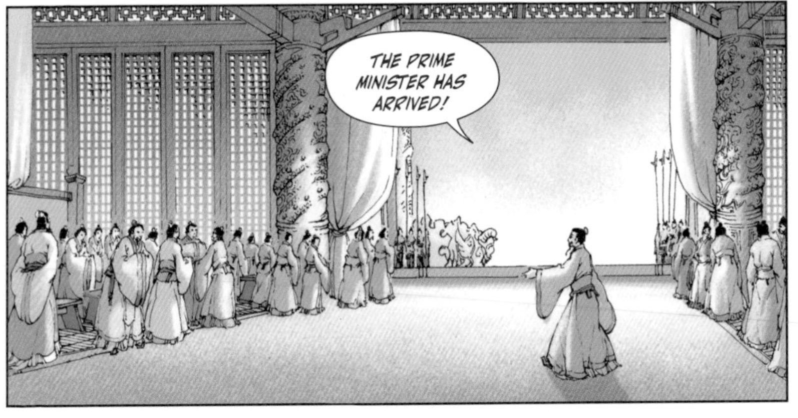
THE PRIME MINISTER HAS ARRIVED!

BEI LIU, MAY I PRESENT CHENG DONG, A TRUSTED ADVISOR.
AND OVER HERE...

MEET RONG KONG FROM BEIHAI. I BELIEVE YOU'VE MET BEFORE.

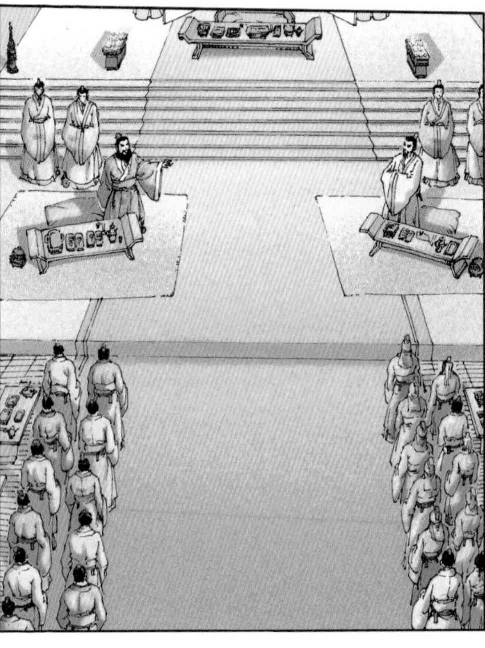

HIS MAJESTY HAS ARRIVED!

EMPEROR XIAN
PLEASE BE SEATED.

BEI LIU CARRIES HIMSELF IN SUCH A DIGNIFIED WAY.

INDEED. HE SEEMS TO PUT THOSE AROUND HIM AT EASE.

WHAT ARE YOU MUMBLING TO YOURSELF?
WHAT? OH, NEVER MIND.

STEP FORWARD, BEI LIU. YOU ARE OF ROYAL BLOOD, AREN'T YOU?
I AM, YOUR HIGH-NESS.
I AM DESCEND-ED FROM EMPEROR XIAO JING.

HM. WE MIGHT HAVE AN ALLY.

IS THIS TRUE? I MUST KNOW...

FETCH ME THE ROYAL FAMILY RECORD!

I BET CAO CAO IS IN A FOUL MOOD TODAY.
WHY?
BIAO YANG

WORD HAS IT THAT BEI LIU'S YOUNGER BROTHER KILLED DIAO CHAN.

YOU MEAN THE BEAUTIFUL MISTRESS WHO GOT ZHUO DONG KILLED?
THAT'S RIGHT. CAO CAO IS A NOTORIOUS WOMAN CHASER. NOW HE WON'T BE ABLE TO CHASE THE PRIZE WHO BROUGHT DOWN HIS DEADLIEST FOE.

HE DOESN'T APPEAR TO BE VERY UPSET ABOUT IT.
JUST THE SAME, I'M SURE HIS BLOOD IS BOILING WITH BEI LIU BY HIS SIDE.

IT'S TRUE! COMMANDER LIU IS A BLOOD RELATIVE!
STEP FORWARD, COMMANDER LIU.

YOU ARE MY UNCLE BY DESCENT. LET ME CALL YOU THAT FROM NOW ON.

THE HONOR IS MORE THAN I DESERVE, YOUR MAJESTY!
NO HONOR IS TOO GREAT FOR A HERO LIKE YOU.

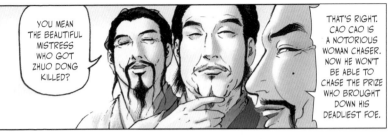

YOU ARE TOO MODEST FOR YOUR OWN GOOD, BEI LIU.
HE'S RIGHT. AND DON'T FORGET, THERE'S A FINE LINE BETWEEN MODESTY AND HYPOCRISY.

YOUR HIGHNESS, IT BRINGS US GREAT JOY TO SEE YOU IN THE COMPANY OF FAMILY AFTER ALL THIS TIME.
CONGRATULATIONS, YOUR MAJESTY!

HM.
VERY CLEVER. THEIRS IS A SLY GAME...

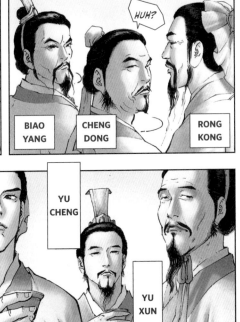

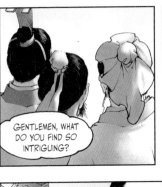

GENTLEMEN, WHAT DO YOU FIND SO INTRIGUING?

YU CHENG

JIA GUO

YU XUN

OH, THE THREE OF YOU STARTLED US! HOW ARE YOU?

THE QUESTION IS, HOW ARE *YOU?* YOU LOOK TROUBLED.

TROUBLED?
NOT AT ALL! THE EMPEROR HAS BEEN REUNITED WITH A FAMILY MEMBER. WE ARE DEEPLY MOVED, THAT'S ALL.

MOVED. I SEE...

WHAT ABOUT YOU, JIA GUO? STILL FIGHTING WITH YU XUN?
OR HAVE THE TWO OF YOU KISSED AND MADE UP?

RUMORS OF A FEUD ARE ABSURD.
WE ARE ROYAL SUBJECTS OF THE HAN DYNASTY. WE DON'T BOTHER WITH PETTY FIGHTS.

ROYAL SUBJECTS OF THE HAN DYNASTY?
I THOUGHT YOU WERE *LOYAL SERVANTS* OF CAO CAO.

WELL...

PRIME MINISTER CAO IS A ROYAL OFFICIAL, SO SERVING HIM MEANS SERVING THE DYNASTY, OF COURSE.
WE SHOULD BE GOING NOW.

HUH.

THERE ARE RATS IN THE PALACE, AND THEY ARE USING CAO CAO FOR COVER.
I WON'T SIT BACK AND ALLOW THIS TO HAPPEN.

LATER THAT DAY, CAO CAO GATHERED WITH HIS ADVISORS.

SO...

I WAS RIGHT.

THOSE LISTED HERE DO NOT CARE FOR ME AT ALL, DO THEY?

NO, MY LORD. AND WHEN THE TIME COMES, THEY WILL BETRAY YOU.
I SEE.

BIAO YANG, CHENG DONG, AND RONG KONG ARE THE CENTRAL PLAYERS.
OF THEM, BIAO YANG IS THE MOST ARROGANT.

AND RONG KONG THE MOST CUNNING.
HE'S THE ONE WHO RECRUITS OTHERS TO THEIR CAUSE.

THE PROBLEM IS THAT IF WE CONFRONT THESE ROYAL ADVISORS DIRECTLY, WE RISK LOSING FAVOR WITH THE PUBLIC.

ROYAL ADVISORS?
WHEN EXACTLY HAVE THEY ADVISED?
I RECALL BEING THE ONE WHO FOUGHT THE BATTLES...

...AND SAVED PEOPLE.
WHILE I WAS DOING THAT, THEY TALKED MUCH AND ACHIEVED NOTHING!

WHAT DO YOU PLAN TO DO?

WHAT I SHOULD HAVE DONE THEN. *I'LL WIPE THEM OUT!*
BUT, MY LORD...

YES, STRIKE THEM DOWN AT ONCE.

NO! REMEMBER, A DOG CAN BE MADE OBEDIENT WHETHER YOU BEAT HIM OR FEED HIM.

SOMETIMES REWARD IS MORE EFFECTIVE THAN PUNISHMENT.

I DIS-AGREE, MY LORD.
THESE MEN ARE BOTH COWARDLY AND USELESS. I SAY WE GET RID OF THEM AS A WARNING TO THE OTHERS. NO ONE WILL PLOT AGAINST YOU THEN.

HM...

I AGREE. BUT I NEED YOU TWO TO AGREE ON THIS.
IF YOU SUPPORT WHAT I'M ABOUT TO SAY, DO SO IN UNISON.

I WILL GET RID OF BIAO YANG AS SOON AS I HAVE THE CHANCE. SO WE MUST BE READY. AGREED?
AGREED.

SEE? THAT WASN'T SO HARD. I LIKE IT WHEN YOU TWO ARE OF THE SAME MIND.
HA HA HA!
HA HA HA!
PRETTY SOON, I WON'T BE ABLE TO TELL THE TWO OF YOU APART!

LATER ON, BEI LIU MET WITH THE EMPEROR…
UNCLE, I WANTED TO SPEAK WITH YOU IN PRIVATE.
I'M HAPPY TO OBLIGE, YOUR MAJESTY.

TELL ME, HOW DO YOU TRULY FEEL ABOUT CAO CAO?
!

WHAT IF I TOLD YOU HE WAS A TRAITOR AND A THREAT TO MY THRONE AND LIFE?

THEN I WOULD GLADLY RISK MY LIFE TO CUT OFF THIS TRAITOR'S HEAD AND PRESENT IT TO YOU AS A GIFT.
THMP

I BEG YOU, DEAR UNCLE.
SAVE ME, AND THE DYNASTY, FROM THE CLUTCHES OF THIS VILLAIN.

YOUR MAJESTY, I WILL DRIVE HIM FROM THIS LAND NO MATTER THE COST. LEAVE IT TO ME, AND DON'T REVEAL WHAT WE'VE SPOKEN OF TO ANYONE.

THANK THE HEAVENS! YOU CAN'T IMAGINE WHAT A RELIEF IT IS TO HEAR THAT. FOR TOO LONG, I'VE BEEN TREATED LIKE A PUPPET. I CAN'T TAKE IT ANYMORE.

OF COURSE I WON'T.
THANK YOU, UNCLE. I WILL BE PATIENT.
THANK YOU, YOUR MAJESTY.

YOUR MAJESTY, THE PRIME MINISTER HAS ARRIVED.

YOUR MAJ--
OH, HELLO BEI LIU.

ONE MORE THING.
I'VE ARRANGED FOR A HUNTING PARTY TOMORROW.
THAT'S A GOOD POINT.

A HUNTING PARTY? FOR WHAT? THIS IS NOT TIME FOR THAT.

IT IS TRADITION FOR THE EMPEROR TO LEAD A HUNTING PARTY ONCE A SEASON. IT SHOWS STRENGTH.
AND GIVEN HOW ANXIOUS THE PEOPLE HAVE BECOME, THEY WOULD WELCOME A SHOW OF STRENGTH.

YES, BUT I'M THE ONE WHO DECIDES THESE THINGS! YOU DO NOT GIVE ME ORDERS ON SUCH THINGS.

!

YOUR MAJESTY, IF I MAY: I THINK THIS WOULD HELP GET YOUR MIND OFF OF THINGS.
LET YOU CLEAR YOUR HEAD A BIT.

SIGH...

ALL RIGHT.
I WILL GO ALONG WITH YOUR IDEA.

NYEH
CLOP CLOP CLOP
ARF ARF
ARF
!
HOOSH

SHOON

WHOMP
IT'S A GOLDEN ARROW...
HURRAH!
THIS IS THE EMPEROR'S ARROW!
HURRAH! LONG LIVE THE EMPEROR!

WELL?

YOUR ARROW FOUND ITS MARK!
LONG LIVE YOUR MAJESTY!

...
NYEH!

HERE
HERE!

I DON'T MEAN TO RUIN THE MOOD, BUT I'M THE ONE WHO SHOT THE ARROW.

HIS MAJESTY DIDN'T EVEN REALIZE HE WAS MISSING AN ARROW FROM HIS QUIVER.

YOUR ARCHERY SKILLS ARE BEYOND COMPARE, MY LORD.
WE'RE GLAD YOU'RE THE ONE CARRYING THE BOW!

HA HA HA!

HM...

WHAT A LOWLIFE!
THAT'S IT!
FOOMP
SHOO-

STAND DOWN. BOTH OF YOU. NOW IS NOT THE TIME.
HUH?
CONGRATULA-TIONS, MY LORD.
YOU ARE A MASTER ARCHER IF EVER I'VE SEEN ONE.

HA HA! I CANNOT GIVE ENOUGH CREDIT TO THE EMPEROR'S BOW. WHAT A TREASURE!

YOUR MAJESTY, SINCE YOU HAVE NO INTEREST IN HUNTING, PERHAPS I WILL JUST KEEP THE BOW.

VERY WELL.
HA HA! BACK TO THE PALACE!

HA HA HA!

Fei Zhang

ANSWER ME!
WHY DID YOU STOP ME?

YOU SAW THE WAY THAT ARROGANT FOOL EMBARRASSED THE EMPEROR! IF WE DON'T DO SOMETHING SOON, WE'LL ALL BE BOWING TO A WORTHLESS GUTTER RAT!
WHAM
YEESH. THAT WAS BLUNT.

THEN WHAT ARE WE WAITING FOR? WE NEED TO DEAL WITH THIS *RIGHT NOW!*

I...

TELL ME THIS:
YOU TWO WOULD DIE FOR ME, IS THAT RIGHT?

OF COURSE WE WOULD! WHAT KIND OF QUESTION IS THAT?

WELL, I DON'T NEED YOU TO DIE FOR ME. BUT I NEED YOU TO LIVE AS IF THAT WERE THE CASE.

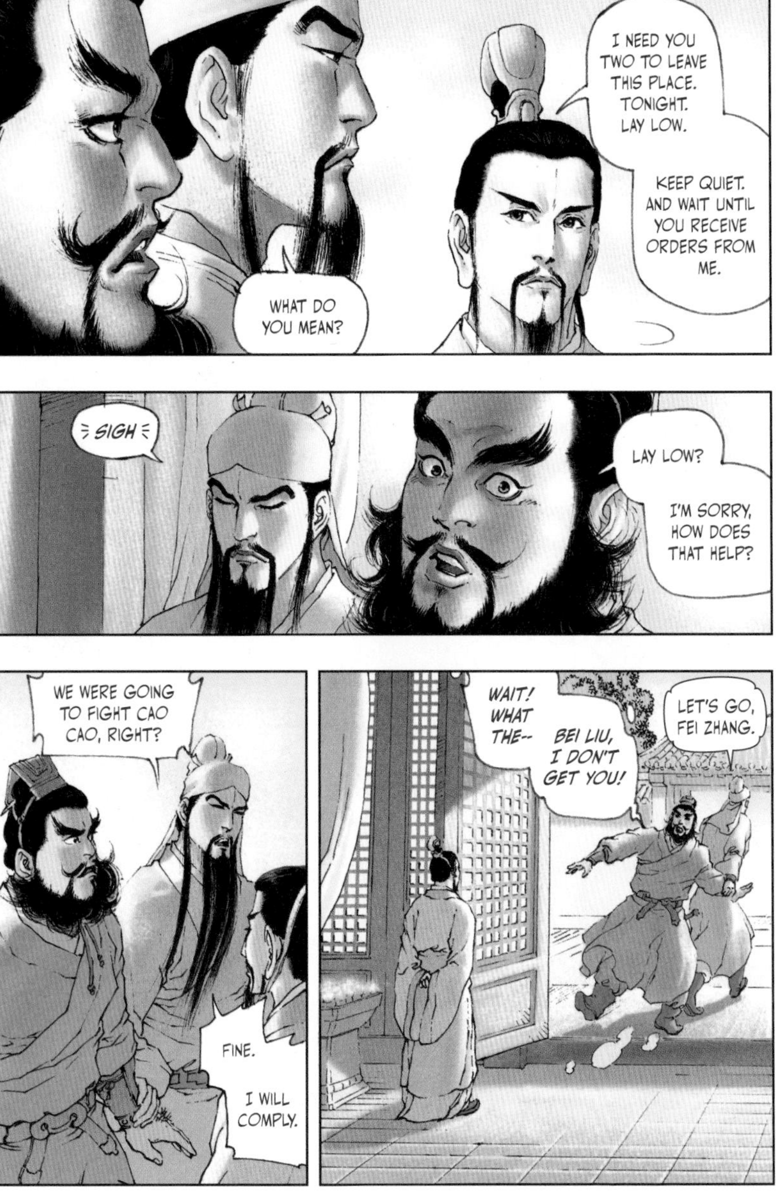
I NEED YOU TWO TO LEAVE THIS PLACE. TONIGHT. LAY LOW.
KEEP QUIET. AND WAIT UNTIL YOU RECEIVE ORDERS FROM ME.
WHAT DO YOU MEAN?
LAY LOW?
I'M SORRY, HOW DOES THAT HELP?
SIGH
WE WERE GOING TO FIGHT CAO CAO, RIGHT?
FINE.
I WILL COMPLY.
LET'S GO, FEI ZHANG.
WAIT! WHAT THE--
BEI LIU, I DON'T GET YOU!

LATER, CHENG DONG INVITED BEI LIU TO HIS RESIDENCE FOR A DRINK...
≡ BURP ≡ OKAY, ENOUGH.
I CAN'T DRINK ANY MORE TONIGHT.

I'D BETTER GET GOING NOW.

HANG ON, BEI LIU.
SLAP

IT'S STILL QUITE EARLY. WON'T YOU STAY JUST A LITTLE LONGER?

IT'S ACTUALLY QUITE LATE.
WHY DON'T YOU GO TO SLEEP?

BECAUSE IT WOULD BE SUCH A SHAME!
I'VE ADMIRED YOU FOR AGES. NOW YOU'RE MY GUEST.

WHY DON'T WE HAVE A NIGHTCAP?

PLEASE. COME INSIDE.
AS YOU WISH.

COME IN, COME IN!

IT'S SO DARK. WHAT'S GOING ON?

KSSHH
!

HA HA HA! DON'T BE SO NERVOUS, BEI LIU. WE'RE JUST INTERESTED IN HAVING A NIGHTCAP.

I AM ZIFU WANG
ZIFU WANG
I AM JI CHONG.
JI CHONG
I AM SHI WU.
THIS IS ZILAN WU
SHI WU
ZILAN WU
TENG MA
I AM TENG MA FROM LIANG XI.
IT'S AN HONOR TO MEET YOU.

PLEASE, SIT DOWN.

THIS SURE DOESN'T LOOK LIKE A DRINKING PARTY.

PERHAPS NOT.
TELL ME, WHAT DO YOU THINK OF CAO CAO?

GET TO THE POINT, AND STOP PLAYING GAMES!
STOP IT!
YOU MUST KNOW HOW HE FEELS!

BEI LIU, PLEASE LOOK AT THIS.

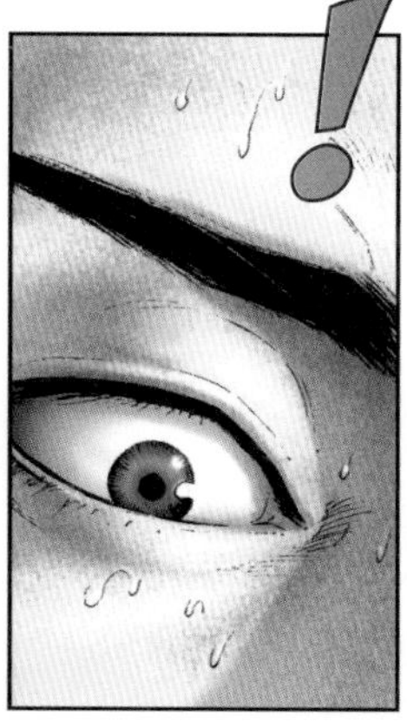

IS THIS?
YES. IT IS A ROYAL ORDER WRITTEN IN THE EMPEROR'S BLOOD.
HE HID IT IN HIS ROBE AND GAVE IT TO CHENG DONG.

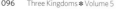

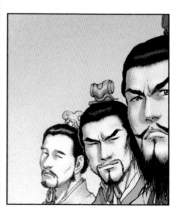

YOU KNOW WHAT THIS MEANS, BEI LIU, SO WE'LL SPARE YOU A LENGTHY EXPLANATION.
WE HAVE PLEDGED IN BLOOD TO DO WHATEVER IT TAKES TO DEFEAT CAO CAO AND RESTORE THE HAN DYNASTY. AND WE WANT YOU TO JOIN OUR PLEDGE, BEI LIU.

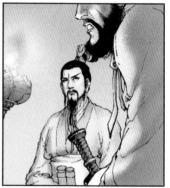

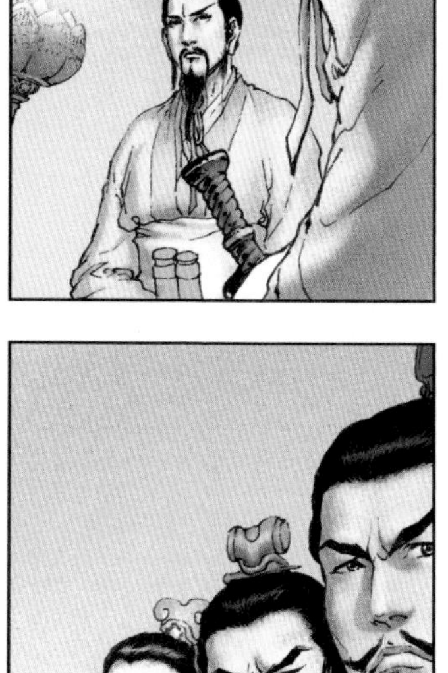

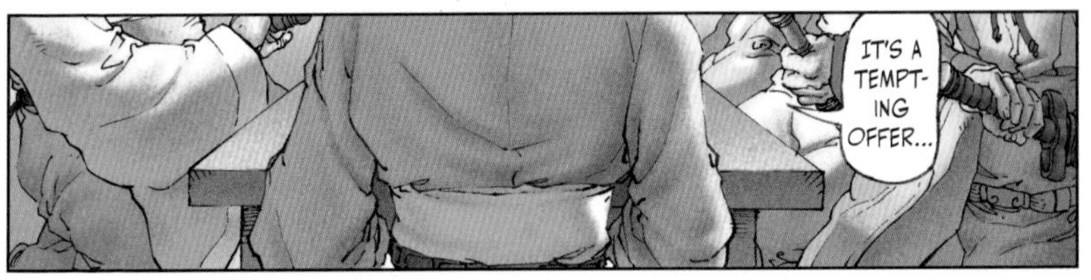
IT'S A TEMPT-ING OFFER...

AND I AM ALREADY ACTING ON SECRET ORDERS TO GET RID OF CAO CAO.

SO I WILL JOIN YOUR PLEDGE. BUT I AM ACCUSTOMED TO WRITING THEM IN MY OWN WAY.

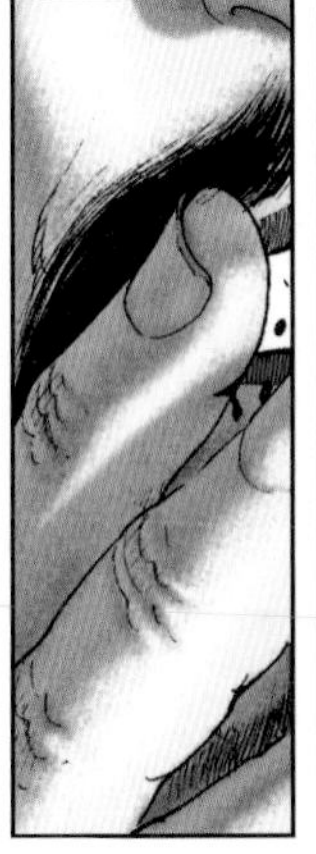

I KNOW I'LL SLEEP BETTER NOW.

NOW WE CAN RISE AGAINST CAO CAO. HAN WILL SOON BE RESTORED!

SO TELL ME...
WHAT'S OUR PLAN FOR HOW TO REVOLT?
THERE'S NOTHING CONCRETE YET.
WELL...

GIVE US A DAY OR SO, AND WE'LL GET BACK TO YOU.
WE'RE STILL WORKING OUT THE DETAILS. BUT WE ARE UNITED!

≡ SIGH ≡
ALL RIGHT, HOW ABOUT THIS?

HOW ABOUT I GO DIRECTLY TO CAO CAO RIGHT NOW, AND I TELL HIM EXACTLY WHAT WE'VE BEEN TALKING ABOUT HERE TONIGHT?

WHAT? BEI LIU!
HE'S A SPY!

TENG MA! TAKE IT EASY!
THAT MAY NOT BE WHAT HE MEANT.

CALM DOWN, ALL OF YOU! LET'S HEAR WHAT HE HAS TO SAY.

HE DEFEATED BOTH BU LU AND SHU YUAN,
AND IN DOING SO GAINED XUZHOU AND SHOUCHUN.
WHAT I MEANT WAS THAT CAO CAO IS RIDING HIGH THESE DAYS.

PLUS HE HAS COMPLETE CONTROL OVER THE IMPERIAL ARMY.

THAT GIVES HIM A FIGHTING FORCE OF MORE THAN 500,000 SOLDIERS.
NOW, THEY MAY BE SOLDIERS OF THE HAN DYNASTY, BUT THEIR FIDELITY IS TO CAO CAO.
THOSE OF US IN THIS ROOM ARE UNITED, BUT ALL THAT MEANS IS THAT WE'D CHARGE HEADFIRST INTO A BRICK WALL TOGETHER.

BEI LIU, WE ARE NOT A BUNCH OF AMBITIOUS YOUNG NOBLES. I HAVE 10,000 SOLDIERS IN LIANGXI WAITING FOR MY COMMAND!
I KNOW. AND THAT'S NO SMALL ACCOMPLISHMENT, TENG MA.

BUT LIANGXI IS A LONG WAY FROM HERE.
IN THE MEANTIME, WHO WOULD PROTECT THE EMPEROR AND HIS PEOPLE UNTIL YOUR FORCES ARRIVE?

SO...
DO YOU HAVE ANY BETTER IDEAS?
AGAINST AN ENEMY THIS STRONG, THE BEST PLAN IS NOT TO ATTACK, BUT TO OUTLAST. WE SHOULD ALLY OURSELVES WITH CAO CAO.

IT'S THE BEST WAY TO CATCH HIM WITH HIS GUARD DOWN.

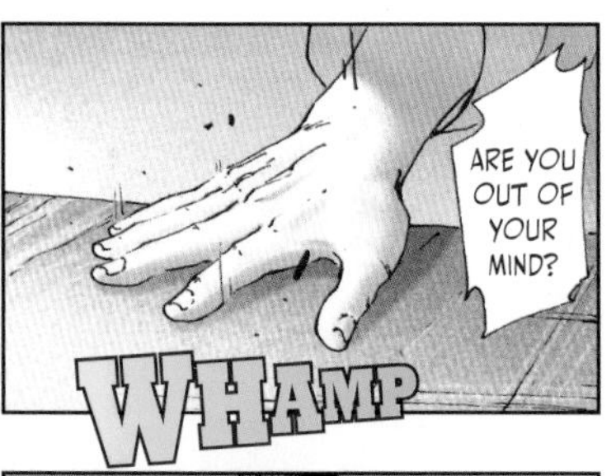
ARE YOU OUT OF YOUR MIND?
WHAMP

I'LL DIE BEFORE I JOIN HIM!
I CANNOT ALLY MYSELF WITH A TRAITOR AND A THIEF. SUCH A DISHONOR WOULD BE WORSE THAN DEATH!

JOIN FORCES WITH CAO CAO?
ARE YOU TRYING TO GET US KILLED?

I ADMIRE YOUR DEVOTION TO PRINCIPLE.
BUT THESE DAYS IT ISN'T ENOUGH. WE NEED A NEW STRATEGY.
SPARE ME THE LECTURE. SINCE WHEN IS GIVING UP A STRATEGY?

ATTACKING CAO CAO DIRECTLY WOULD LEAD TO CERTAIN DEATH. THEN WHO WOULD BE LEFT TO DEAL WITH CAO CAO?
WELL...

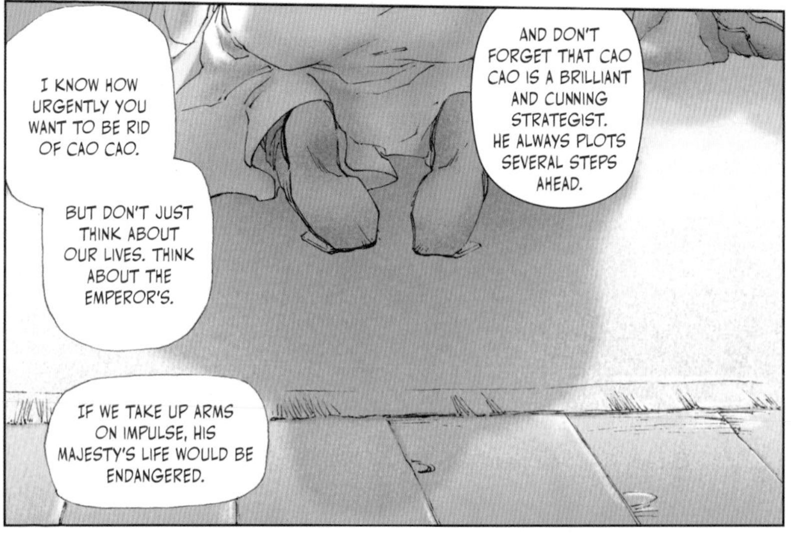
I KNOW HOW URGENTLY YOU WANT TO BE RID OF CAO CAO.
BUT DON'T JUST THINK ABOUT OUR LIVES. THINK ABOUT THE EMPEROR'S.
AND DON'T FORGET THAT CAO CAO IS A BRILLIANT AND CUNNING STRATEGIST. HE ALWAYS PLOTS SEVERAL STEPS AHEAD.
IF WE TAKE UP ARMS ON IMPULSE, HIS MAJESTY'S LIFE WOULD BE ENDANGERED.

OKAY.
WHAT DO YOU SUGGEST WE DO THEN?
I TOLD YOU. WE WAIT.

PATIENCE IS NOT THE SAME THINGS AS HELPLESS-NESS OR SURRENDER.
SOMETIMES WAITING IS THE BEST KIND OF ATTACK.

I SEE.
HOW LONG DO WE HAVE TO WAIT?

WE'LL KNOW THE RIGHT MOMENT WHEN WE SEE IT.

UNTIL THEN, WE REMAIN STOIC AND CALM.
ONLY THEN WILL CAO CAO BE VULNERABLE.
LET US PLEDGE THAT THIS CONVERSA-TION REMAINS SECRET.
I DON'T KNOW ABOUT THIS.
YOU KNOW, VOLCANOES CAN LIE DORMANT FOR HUNDREDS OF YEARS, BUT NO ONE QUESTIONS THEIR STRENGTH, BECAUSE ONCE THEY ERUPT THEY CAN BLOW APART A MOUNTAIN. WHEN THE TIME IS RIGHT, SO CAN WE.

I BID YOU GOOD NIGHT.

KLANSH

WHAT WAS THAT?!

I'LL CHECK IT OUT.

HOOT HOOT

IT'S NOTHING. THERE WAS A SLEEPING SERVANT NEXT DOOR. HE KNOCKED SOMETHING OVER.
DO YOU THINK HE HEARD US TALKING?

I DON'T THINK SO.
BUT WE'D BETTER GET OUT OF HERE, JUST IN CASE.

BEI LIU, YOU GO OUT THE FRONT GATE.
THE FIVE OF US WILL GO OUT THE BACK.

KREEK

Chapter 3

Cao Cao and Bei Liu: A Battle of Wits AD 199

Summary

Bei Liu withdraws from the business of the kingdom and feigns indifference to world affairs while tending a vegetable garden at his home. One day, he is summoned to the palace by Cao Cao's soldiers. At first Bei Liu thinks he is under arrest; however, Cao Cao has invited him for a drink and a conversation. During the conversation, Cao Cao tests Bei Liu with a series of questions designed to reveal Bei Liu's true allegiance. Bei Liu is slightly uncomfortable, but he blames it on the rolling thunder in the distance. Their conversation is interrupted, first by Bei Liu's brothers, then by the news that Shao Yuan invaded the lands of Zan GongSun, who killed himself to avoid capture. Now, Shao Yuan's brother, Shu, wants to give him the emperor's royal seal and form an alliance. Knowing that such an alliance will cause problems for Cao Cao, Bei Liu offers to take an army and ambush Shu Yuan. Cao Cao's advisors question the wisdom of giving Bei Liu an army, but Cao Cao is aware of the danger.

Shu Yuan suffers a humiliating defeat at the hands of Bei Liu and dies by choking on his own blood. One of Shu Yuan's men takes the royal seal and sets out to present it to Cao Cao, while Bei Liu remains in XuZhou, waiting for his moment to strike.

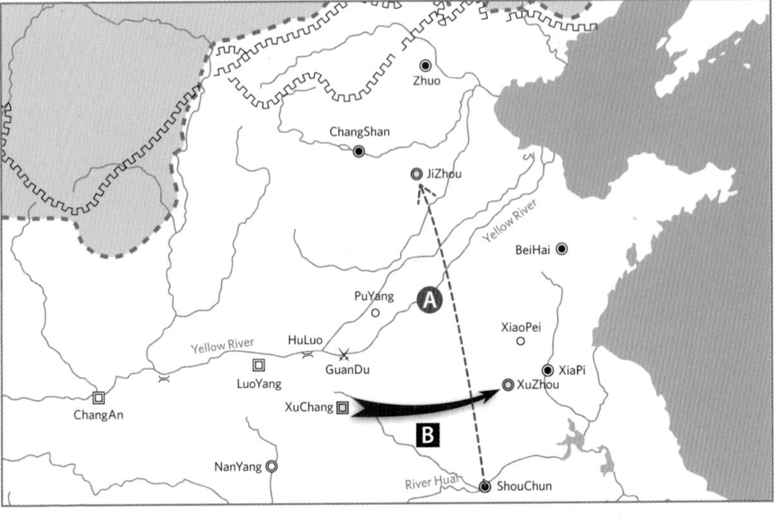

A Having lost most of his army and his power, Shu Yuan tries to form an alliance with his brother by offering him the emperor's royal seal.

B Bei Liu, looking for an opportunity to break out from under Cao Cao's thumb, takes an army to attack Shu Yuan as he tries to deliver the seal to his brother.

The Death of Shu Yuan

Shu Yuan is in possession of the Emperor's Hereditary Seal, a powerful symbol of royalty. When he received the seal, he withdrew from combat and lived an opulent lifestyle financed by the taxes he levied on his own people. Many of his subjects fled the territory, and Shu Yuan's power waned. As the situation worsened, Shu Yuan asked his brother Shao to form an alliance with him, offering the royal seal in return. Now, as Shu Yuan makes his way toward JiZhou, he is attacked by Bei Liu, who leads an army of Cao Cao's soldiers to defeat him. Shu Yuan is a victim of the corrupting influence of power, or even the perception of power: he was not royalty, yet the seal was powerful enough to delude him into thinking that he was.

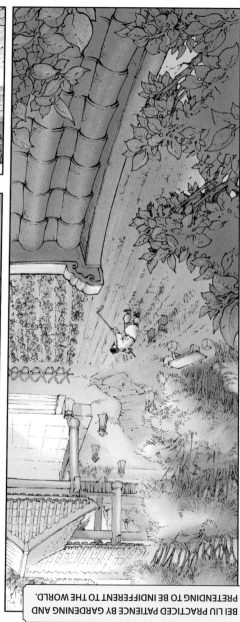

BEI LIU PRACTICED PATIENCE BY GARDENING AND PRETENDING TO BE INDIFFERENT TO THE WORLD.

MY LORD!
YOU NEED TO COME TO THE GATE!
THERE ARE A BUNCH OF CAO CAO'S SOLDIERS OUTSIDE.

SOL-
DIERS?

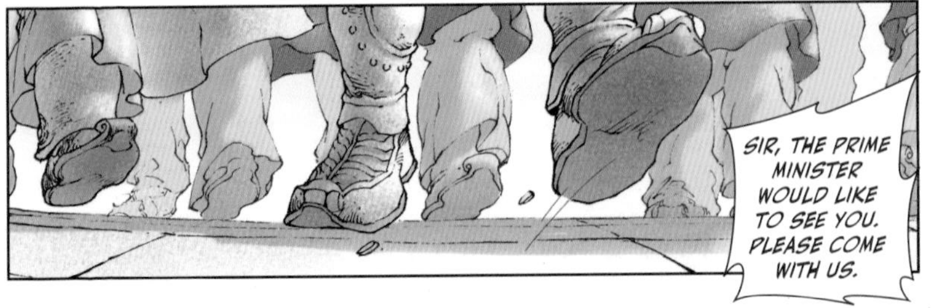
SIR, THE PRIME MINISTER WOULD LIKE TO SEE YOU. PLEASE COME WITH US.

CHU XU
LIAO ZHANG

FORGIVE US, COMMANDER BEI LIU, WE'VE BEEN GIVEN A DIRECT ORDER TO BRING YOU IN.

DID HE SAY WHY HE WANTS TO SEE ME? AM I UNDER ARREST?

NO. WE WERE TOLD ONLY THAT HE WANTS TO SEE YOU.

HA HA! FORGIVE ME.
IT'S NOT EVERY DAY A GROUP OF ARMED SOLDIERS SHOWS UP AT MY DOOR.

I THOUGHT YOU HAD COME TO TAKE ME IN BY ANY MEANS NECESSARY.

NOT AT ALL.

YOU ARE A BLOOD RELATIVE OF THE EMPEROR.
YOU DESERVE TO BE GUARDED BY HIS SOLDIERS.

HA! THIS IS FAR BETTER TREATMENT THAN I DESERVE. JUST THE SAME, I WILL GO ALONG WITH YOU. LET ME CHANGE MY CLOTHES...

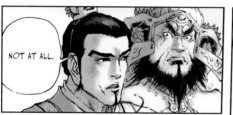

HELLO, BEI LIU.

YOU'RE A HARD MAN TO FIND THESE DAYS.

I HEAR YOU ARE CONFINING YOURSELF TO HOME AND WORKING ON SOMETHING AMBITIOUS.

!

IT'S FUNNY TO THINK A HERO SUCH AS YOURSELF HAS PUT ALL OF HIS ENERGY INTO CREATING CHINA'S FINEST VEGETABLE GARDEN.

PHEW...
HE DOESN'T KNOW.
I MAY HAVE ROYAL BLOOD, BUT I HAD A PEASANT'S UPBRINGING. GARDENING SOOTHES ME. I HOPE YOU WON'T LAUGH AT ME.

HA HA HA! LAUGH AT YOU?
I DIDN'T BRING YOU HERE TO LAUGH AT YOU.

YOU KNOW, I WAS WALKING THROUGH AN APRICOT FOREST RECENTLY. IT REMINDED ME OF A TIME WHEN I REMEDIED THIRSTY SOLDIERS BY TELLING THEM THERE WAS A LUSCIOUS APRICOT FOREST NEARBY.

THE THOUGHT MADE THEIR MOUTHS WATER SO MUCH THAT THEIR THIRST WAS QUENCHED.
HA HA! VERY CLEVER, MY LORD.

I'VE BEEN THINKING ABOUT THE PAST LATELY. HENCE I THOUGHT OF YOU.

I HAVEN'T SEEN YOU IN AGES, SO I INVITED YOU TO SHARE SOME PLUM WINE WITH ME.
I'M HONORED. THANK YOU.

≡ GULP ≡
AH! LET'S GO AGAIN!
BOTTOMS UP!
HAHAHA!

SO, BEI LIU, WHAT KIND OF RUMORS HAVE YOU HEARD LATELY?
NONE. I'M TOO BUSY GARDENING.

I SEE.
WELL, SOME OF MY ADVISORS WANT TO KILL ME.
⋛ GULP ⋚ IS THAT SO?

WHO THINKS THEY CAN GET AWAY WITH SUCH A THING?

HA HA! CALM DOWN, BEI LIU. I'M AWARE OF THE PLOT AND WILL TRACK DOWN THE OFFENDERS ONE BY ONE IF I HAVE TO.
VERY GOOD, MY LORD. YOU ARE MOST WISE.

THANK YOU. YOU KNOW, I'VE HEARD THAT SOME PEOPLE COMPARE ME TO BU LU.

THAT'S ABSURD! YOU GOVERN WITH KINDNESS AND WISDOM. BU LU KNEW ONLY BRUTE FORCE.

VERY TRUE.
IT'S GOOD TO BE ABLE TO TALK TO SOMEONE WHO UNDERSTANDS.
MY INTENTION IS TO BRING AN END TO THIS VIOLENT AGE AND USHER IN A TIME OF PEACE.
AND I WANT YOU TO HELP ME DO IT.

REJOIN MY RANKS, AND NOTHING WILL BE IMPOSSIBLE!

YOUR PRAISE IS MOST APPRECIATED. BUT I'M AFRAID THOSE DAYS ARE BEHIND ME.
NOW I'M JUST A HUMBLE FARMER.

I OWE IT ALL TO YOU, OF COURSE. WITHOUT YOU, I'D BE DEAD BY NOW.

HA HA HA HA!
SUCH MODESTY!

RUMBLE

TELL ME, BEI LIU, WHAT DO YOU KNOW ABOUT DRAGONS?
NOT AS MUCH AS I SHOULD, I'M AFRAID.

KRASHOOM

THE DRAGON IS THE MIGHTIEST CREATURE IN ALL OF CREATION. IT MOVES FURIOUSLY AND WITHOUT DANGER OVER LAND, SEA, AND AIR. BUT IT ALSO CLOAKS ITSELF IN A FOG OF SMOKE, SO THAT ENEMIES CANNOT SEE IT.
THE DRAGONS OF LEGEND AND THE GREAT MEN OF TODAY HAVE THAT IN COMMON. THEY MOVE SWIFTLY AND WITH GREAT STEALTH.

LET'S TALK FOR A MOMENT ABOUT TODAY'S GREAT MEN...

I'M AFRAID I DON'T KNOW TOO MANY.

DON'T BE SILLY.
SPEAK YOUR MIND.
WELL...

SHU YUAN HAS BUILT A TREMENDOUS ARMY IN THE SOUTH, AND HE HAS PROVIDED FOR HIS PEOPLE. HE COULD BE A GREAT MAN.

SHU YUAN IS A ROTTING HUSK. SOON I'LL BE ABLE TO CHOP HIM DOWN.

HIS BROTHER, SHAO YUAN OF THE NORTH, IS DESCENDED FROM A NOBLE FAMILY AND HAS A POWERFUL TEAM OF COMMANDERS AND ADVISORS. I SUPPOSE HE'S ONE OF THE GREATS.

ON THE SURFACE, PERHAPS.
BUT SHAO YUAN IS A RAT. HE CAN SCHEME, BUT HE CANNOT DECIDE OR LEAD.
HE RISKS HIS LIFE TO RESOLVE TRIVIAL MATTERS AND PETTY GRIEVANCES, BUT HE HIDES WHENEVER SOMETHING IMPORTANT COMES UP. I DO NOT CONSIDER HIM GREAT.

AND WHAT ABOUT CE SUN? HIS EXPLOITS ARE AWE-INSPIRING.

THERE'S SHOU ZHANG AND SHOU HAN IN THE WEST. SURELY THEY--

HM.

HE OWES HIS SUCCESS TO HIS FATHER'S MEMORY.

THEY ARE NOT WORTH TALKING ABOUT.

WORTHLESS, BOTH OF THEM.

I SEE.

WELL, I'M AFRAID I'VE RUN OUT OF NAMES.

LISTEN, BEI LIU...

A GREAT MAN IS AN ALMOST IMPOSSIBLE COMBINATION OF THINGS. A NOBLE HEART, A CUNNING MIND, AND THE ABILITY TO SEE THE REASON OF THE UNIVERSE.

DO YOU REALLY THINK SUCH A PERSON EVEN EXISTS?

I SHOULD CERTAINLY HOPE SO.
YOU AND I CAN'T BE THE ONLY GREAT MEN IN THE WHOLE WORLD, CAN WE? *HA HA!*

!
KRING
BAROOOM
KRACK

I'M SORRY. THE THUNDER STARTLED ME.

YOU KNOW, A GREAT MAN WOULDN'T BE STARTLED BY THUNDER.
MY LORD, I THINK THE GODS THEMSELVES WERE STARTLED BY THAT.

STOP RIGHT THERE! HOW DARE YOU TRESPASS?

OOF!
STEP ASIDE! WE'RE HERE TO SEE BEI LIU.

BROTHER!

* Hong-Men Party: In 206 BC, a drinking party was held by Yu Xiang and Bang Liu, who fought for supremacy at the end of the Qin Dynasty. Their two generals performed a sword dance, during which Bang Liu's general tried to kill Yu Xiang, whose own general stopped him.

HEY! YOU'RE NOT SUPPOS-ED TO BE IN HERE!
CHONG MAN
GET OUT OF MY WAY!
WHAT IS IT?
MY LORD! I HAVE AN URGENT MESSAGE.
I, UM...

NOW SHU YUAN, WHO'S OTHERWISE POWERLESS, WANTS TO GIVE HIS BROTHER THE EMPEROR'S ROYAL SEAL.

IF THOSE TWO JOIN FORCES, WE ARE GOING TO HAVE SERIOUS PROBLEMS.

MY LORD! SHU YUAN WILL HAVE TO PASS THROUGH XUZHOU TO REACH HIS BROTHER. GIVE ME SOME SOLDIERS, AND I'LL LEAD AN AMBUSH AND CAPTURE HIM.

THAT'S TRUE.

GOOD! BECAUSE I WAS ABOUT TO ASK YOU TO DO JUST THAT. TAKE SOME SOLDIERS. PUT MY MIND AT EASE.
HUH.
YOU'D DO THAT FOR ME?

I WON'T FAIL YOU, MY LORD.
I KNOW YOU WON'T.
I HAVE COM-PLETE TRUST IN YOU.

BESIDES, WITH YOUR BROTHERS HERE, SHU YUAN WILL BE NO MATCH FOR YOU.

MY BROTHERS ARE COURA-GEOUS, THIS IS TRUE. BUT I WORRY THAT I'VE LOST MY TACTICAL EDGE.
OH, WILL YOU STOP IT WITH THE MODESTY!
YOU ARE AN INTELLIGENT PERSON. YOU WILL PREVAIL!

I WILL SPEAK WITH THE EMPEROR THIS EVENING. BY
MORNING, YOU WILL HAVE COMMAND OF 50,000 TROOPS READY TO DEPART RIGHT AWAY.

ALL RIGHT, YOU'RE GOING TO HAVE TO EXPLAIN THIS TO ME. WHY ARE WE RISKING OUR NECKS FOR CAO CAO?

BECAUSE OUR MOMENT HAS COME!

DON'T YOU GET IT?

WE'VE BEEN BIDING OUR TIME FOR AGES NOW, WAITING FOR OUR CHANCE. BUT WE'RE OUT OF OUR CAGES NOW, AND IT'S TIME FOR US TO FLY!

Yu Guan

MY LORD, WE SHOULDN'T WALK WITHOUT GUARDS. THE STREETS AREN'T SAFE.

DON'T BE NAIVE. IN AN AGE AS CHAOTIC AS THIS ONE, THERE IS NO SUCH THING AS A SAFE PLACE FOR SOMEONE LIKE ME.

SPEAKING OF WHICH, I'M WORRIED ABOUT BEI LIU.
GIVING HIM AN ARMY IS LIKE THROWING OIL ON A FIRE.

HEY!
LOOK, A WOODEN SWORD!

I USED TO PLAY WITH THESE AS A CHILD!

MY FRIENDS AND I WOULD DIVIDE INTO TWO TEAMS AND FIGHT UNTIL THE SUN WENT DOWN.

HOW TIME FLIES...

MY LORD, ARE YOU LISTENING TO ME?
BEI LIU ACTS LOYAL, BUT I BELIEVE HE'S PLOTTING SOMETHING BEHIND YOUR BACK.

HEY! EITHER BUY IT OR SET IT DOWN!

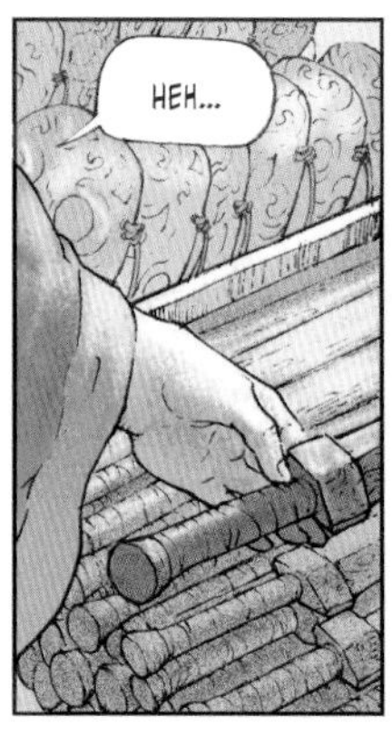
HEH...

MY LORD! YOU MUST LISTEN TO WHAT WE'RE SAYING!

IT IS A GRAVE MISTAKE TO TRUST BEI LIU. HE ACTS MODESTLY, BUT HIS AMBITIONS KNOW NO BOUNDS.

JIA GUO, YU XUN.
DON'T YOU THINK I ALREADY KNOW WHAT YOU'RE TELLING ME?
DON'T YOU THINK I KNOW BEI LIU BETTER THAN YOU?

IT TAKES ONE TO KNOW ONE. I'VE CONSIDERED BEI LIU A RIVAL FROM THE BEGINNING.
WE ARE DESTINED TO VIE FOR THE THRONE.

IF HE'S SUCH A THREAT TO YOU,
WHY DO YOU KEEP HIM AROUND?

LET ME ASK YOU SOMETHING, YU XUN. WHAT GOOD WOULD IT DO ME TO KILL HIM NOW?

NOW I CAN UNDERSTAND WHAT YOU MEAN.

IT DOES NOT HELP MY GOAL TO WIPE OUT SOMEONE WHO, AT THE MOMENT, IS PRACTICALLY POWERLESS.
THE KEY TO REALIZ-ING MY AMBITION IS TO ALWAYS BE ONE STEP AHEAD OF HIM. BEI LIU IS AMBITIOUS,
AND HE WILL ACHIEVE MANY GREAT THINGS. HOWEVER, HE IS NOWHERE NEAR STRONG ENOUGH TO DEFEAT ME, AND HE KNOWS IT. SO HE'LL BE CLEVER.

BUT A DRAGON DOESN'T FIGHT HIS OWN KIND. INSTEAD, HE USES HIS WITS TO OUTSMART THE HEAVENS HE ONE DAY PLANS TO RULE.

IF I KEEP MY WITS ABOUT ME AND STAY ONE STEP AHEAD, I HAVE NO TRUE RIVAL.

AND WINNING THE THRONE WILL REQUIRE OUT-SMARTING, NOT KILLING, THE OPPOSITION.

IF I GET THERE FIRST, BEI LIU AND EVERYONE ELSE WILL KNEEL BEFORE ME.
I SEE WHAT YOU'RE DOING. BUT WHAT HAPPENS IF BEI LIU JOINS FORCES WITH SHAO YUAN?

YES, BUT CLEVER IS OFTEN BETTER THAN STRONG.

MY CONCERNS NOW ARE WELL BEYOND WHATEVER THOSE TWO WOULD MANAGE TO PLOT TOGETHER.

IF BEI CHOOSES THAT ROUTE, THEN HE IS MERELY A WORM, NOT A DRAGON.
HAHAHA!
THEY ARE MERELY TWO SLIMY BEINGS WHO DON'T ALWAYS AGREE ON THINGS.

SHU YUAN, AFTER BEING DEFEATED BY BEI LIU
SHU YUAN
IS THIS...IS THIS JUST WATER?

PLEASE. FIND ME SOME HONEYED WATER.

HONEYED WATER?

ENOUGH!

THERE IS NO HONEYED WATER! THERE IS ONLY BLOOD!
SNAP OUT OF IT!

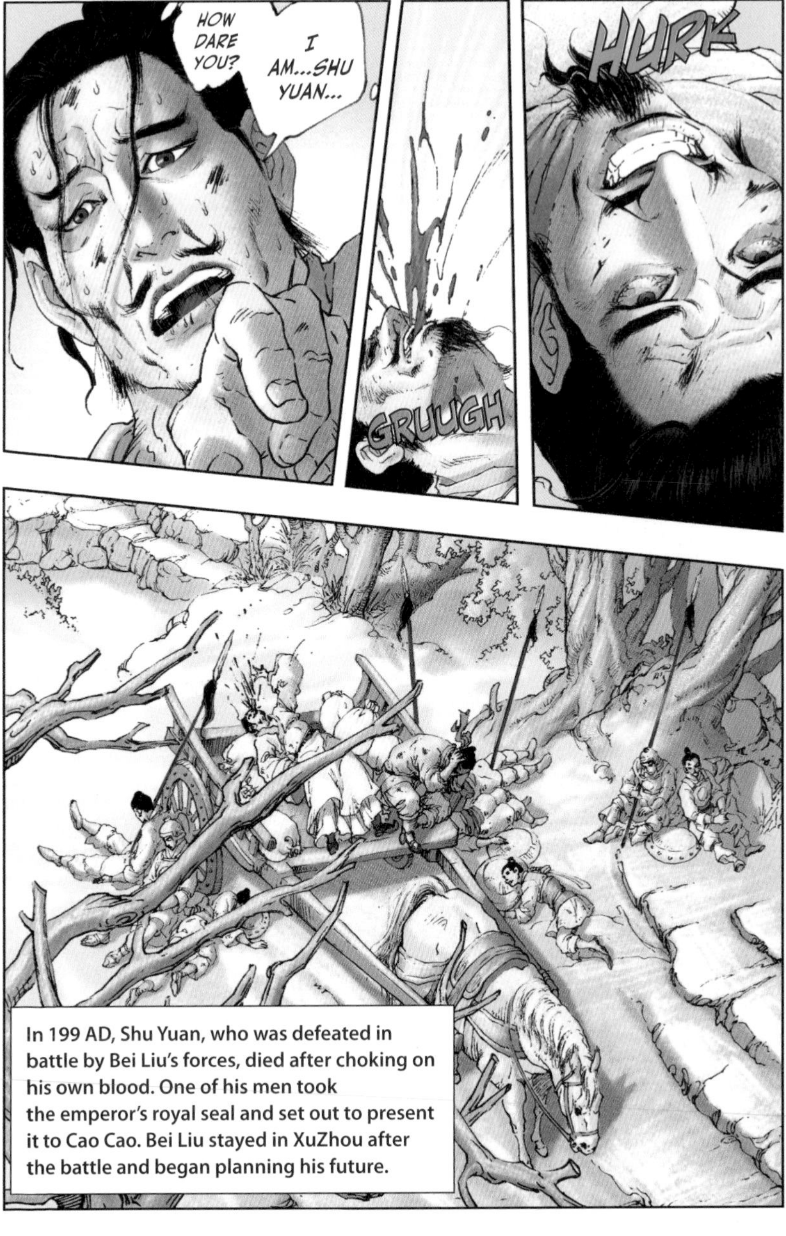
HOW DARE YOU?
I AM...SHU YUAN...
GRUUGH
HURK
In 199 AD, Shu Yuan, who was defeated in battle by Bei Liu's forces, died after choking on his own blood. One of his men took the emperor's royal seal and set out to present it to Cao Cao. Bei Liu stayed in XuZhou after the battle and began planning his future.

Chapter 4

Cao Cao's Killing Spree AD 200

Summary

Thanks to information given to him by one of Cheng Dong's servants, Cao Cao learns of the secret blood oath sworn by the members of the royal court. In retaliation, Cao Cao orders the deaths of more than 800 people, including a royal mistress who is five months pregnant. When he is finished punishing those convicted of treason, he sets his sights on defeating Bei Liu, who has taken root in the city of XuZhou. Bei Liu knows that people will never forgive Cao Cao for his horrific killing spree, and sees this as his chance to take down Cao Cao once and for all. Unfortunately, Bei Liu has nowhere near enough military power to defeat Cao Cao on his own, so he asks Shao Yuan to join him in battle. But Shao Yuan is anything but a reliable person, and Bei Liu could end up paying the ultimate price for putting his trust in someone so untrustworthy.

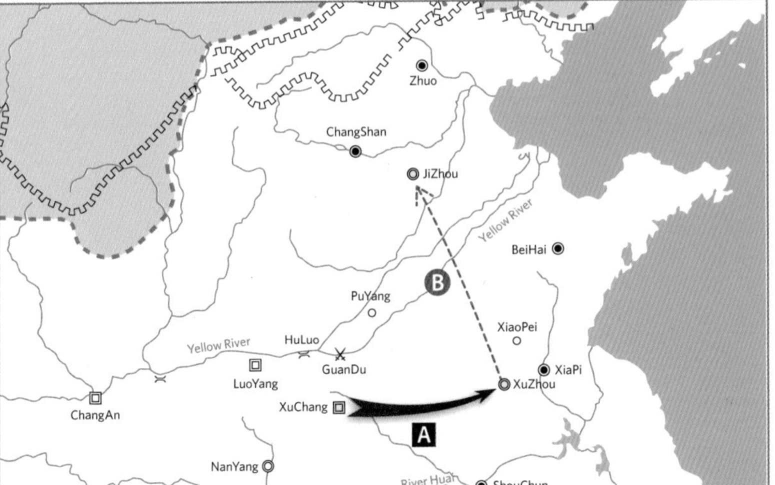

A Cao Cao uncovers a conspiracy against him and executes more than 800 people convicted of treason. He then raises an army of 200,000 soldiers and sets out to attack Bei Liu.

B Bei Liu asks Shao Yuan for aid in fighting Cao Cao's forces. But Shao Yuan is fickle, and at the last moment refuses to come to Bei Liu's aid. Unable to defend XuZhou, Bei Liu flees and takes refuge in Shao Yuan's camp in JiZhou.

The Empress and the Mistress

As was common at the time, Emperor Xian has both a wife and a mistress. His wife is named Empress Shou Fu, and his mistress is named GuiFei Dong. Even though only one woman is legally considered to be the emperor's wife, a child born of either woman can ascend to the throne. Xian himself was the son of a royal mistress when Zhuo Dong crowned him emperor.

CAO CAO'S RESIDENCE, IN XUCHANG
WHO ARE YOU AGAIN?
I AM ONE OF CHENG DONG'S SERVANTS.

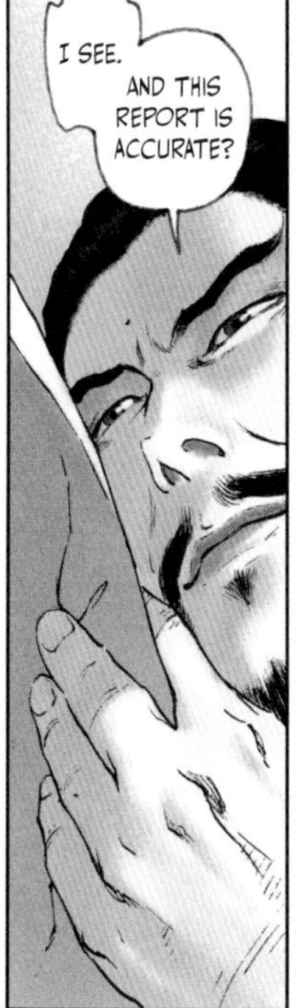
I SEE.
AND THIS REPORT IS ACCURATE?

YES, MY LORD. IT IS ACCURATE.
I HAVE BEEN WORKING FOR CHENG DONG FOR YEARS.

HE NEARLY BEAT ME TO DEATH FOR SPEAKING TO HIS MISTRESS. HE WHIPPED ME AND THREW ME INTO AN EMPTY ROOM.
WHILE I WAS IN THERE, I HEARD CHENG DONG AND OTHERS DISCUSS A CONSPIRACY AGAINST YOU.

I VERY CLEARLY HEARD WHAT THEY WERE TALKING ABOUT.
SEARCH CHENG DONG'S HOME. YOU'LL FIND THEIR PLEDGE, WRITTEN IN BLOOD.

WHAT A CUNNING SERVANT!

WHAT DO YOU THINK OF THIS SITUA-TION?
JIA GUO! YU XUN!

IT'S LIKE THE SAYING GOES.
A TOWER IS ONLY AS STRONG AS ITS WEAKEST STONE.

WELL PUT.
I'LL BET THEY NEVER IMAGINED THAT A MISERABLE LITTLE SERVANT WOULD BRING THEM DOWN.

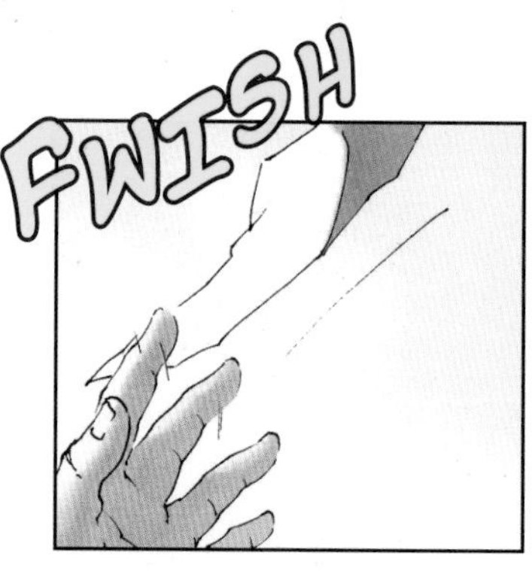

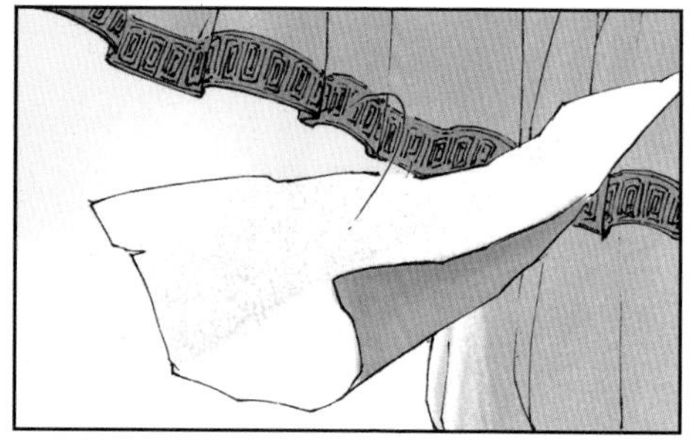

BEI LIU, YOU ARE NOW MORE TROUBLE THAN YOU'RE WORTH.

ARREST EVERY SINGLE MAN LISTED HERE, AND BRING THEM TO ME!

YOU'RE GOING TO REGRET THIS, CAO CAO!
I SWEAR I WILL HAUNT YOU FROM MY GRAVE!
ZIFU WANG
CHENG DONG

JI
CHONG

WELL, MY FRIENDS, DO YOU HAVE ANY LAST WORDS?

SPIT
I DO!
YOU ARE A TRAITOR! AND WHEN YOU DIE, THERE WILL BE A SPECIAL PLACE IN HELL RESERVED JUST FOR YOU!
UNTIL THEN, MY GHOST WILL HAUNT YOUR EVERY WAKING MOMENT!
AND MY FAMILY WILL ENSURE YOUR NAME IS TARNISHED FOREVER!
IS THAT SO?
THEN THERE'S ONLY ONE THING I CAN DO...
GO TO THEIR HOMES AND ROUND UP THEIR FAMILIES.
KILL THEM ALL. EVEN THE WOMEN.

YOU MONSTER!
≡SPIT≡
SPLAT
THEY MADE A PLEDGE BY SMEARING THEIR BLOOD ON WHITE SILK...

HRR!
SHOOMP
≡HUFF≡ NEXT!
THEY PLEDGED TO DEFEND THE EMPEROR...
THEY PLEDGED TO PROTECT THEIR FAMILIES...
NOW THEIR BEST INTENTIONS WILL LIVE IN DISGRACE FOR CENTURIES.

YOUR MAJESTY! I BEG YOU...
SPARE MY LIFE!
THE ROYAL MISTRESS DONG

PLEASE! I'M PREGNANT!

NO!
FOR THE HEAVENS' SAKE, CAO CAO, HAVEN'T YOU KILLED ENOUGH?

I'M SORRY, YOUR MAJESTY, BUT THEY ARE ALL GUILTY.
I AM MERELY CARRYING OUT THE LAWS OF THE LAND.
ROYAL MISTRESS DONG IS CHARGED WITH PLOTTING A REVOLT WITH HER BROTHER CHENG DONG.
THE VERDICT IS GUILTY, THE SEN-TENCE, DEATH.
THIS IS HORRIBLE! THEY'RE GOING TO KILL NINE GENERATIONS OF HER FAMILY!

AS THE CHILD SHE CARRIES BELONGS TO A TRAITOR, IT MUST BE GOTTEN RID OF.

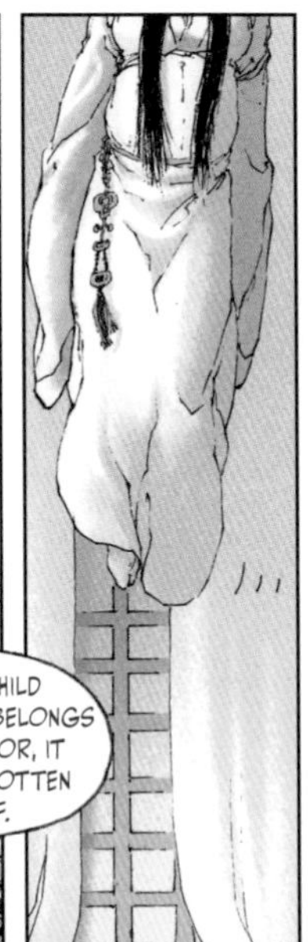

NO!

DAMN YOU, CAO CAO!!!
THE EMPRESS SHOU FU
YOUR MAJESTY! DON'T!

All in all, Cao Cao presided over
the deaths of more than 800 people.
The Royal Mistress Dong,
having been charged with treason,
hanged herself in the royal palace.
She was one of the emperor's
favorite mistresses,
and at the time of her death was
five months pregnant with his child.
IT'S TOO LATE.

THERE! WE'VE EXTRACTED THE POISON FROM WITHIN. NOW WE MUST DESTROY THE OUTSIDE THREAT.
WE SET OUR SIGHTS ON XUZHOU. I WANT BEI LIU'S HEAD ON A PLATE.

Cao Cao

MEANWHILE, IN XUZHOU...

I DON'T BELIEVE THIS...

IT IS A WARNING. IT MEANS MY TURN IS NEXT.

AH, SO THAT'S WHY THERE'S ONE MISSING.
SO, WHAT, YOU'RE SUPPOSED TO GIVE HIM THE FINGER?

FEI ZHANG! THIS IS NO TIME FOR JOKING.

YEAH, BUT I WASN'T KIDDING.
WHAT HAVE I DONE...?
BEI LIU ...

THEY SAY THAT MORE THAN 800 PEOPLE WERE EXECUTED. THEY EVEN KILLED MISTRESS DONG, AND SHE WAS FIVE MONTHS PREGNANT AT THE TIME.

I KNEW AN OPPORTUNITY WOULD PRESENT ITSELF.

THIS IS OUR MOMENT.
WHAT CAO CAO HAS DONE WILL NEVER BE FORGIVEN BY THE PEOPLE. NOW HE CAN BE DEFEATED.
I HAVE ASKED SHAO YUAN TO HELP ME IN BATTLE AGAINST CAO CAO, EVEN THOUGH HE IS SUCH AN INDECISIVE LEADER.

YOU ASKED HIM TO JOIN US AGAINST CAO CAO?
WILL THAT WORK?
SHAO YUAN IS NOT STUPID.
HE MUST KNOW THAT IT'S NOW OR NEVER.

CAO CAO IS LIKELY TO GET HERE BEFORE SHAO YUAN. I DON'T KNOW IF WE CAN HOLD OUT UNTIL HELP ARRIVES.

WE CAN NO LONGER AFFORD TO WORRY ABOUT THINGS LIKE THAT. THIS IS OUR ONE CHANCE TO DEFEAT HIM. WE CAN'T WAIT.

IT IS SAID HE COMMANDS MORE THAN ONE MILLION SOLDIERS.
THEN IT WILL LOOK LIKE A FIELD OF LEAVES SCATTERED IN THE WIND WHEN WE DO BATTLE.
I DO NOT FEAR CAO CAO. I DON'T FEAR THE SIZE OF HIS FIGHTING FORCE. LET US TAKE FLIGHT AT LAST!

≑SIGH≑ I JUST WISH WE COULD DEAL WITH CAO CAO OURSELVES.
I HATE BEING IN A POSITION OF WEAKNESS.

I HATE HAVING TO RELY ON SOMEONE LIKE SHAO YUAN.

MY LORD! I BRING AN URGENT MESSAGE. SHAO YUAN HAS PLEDGED TO RAISE AN ARMY IMMEDIATELY AND ASSIST YOU IN DEFEATING CAO CAO!

HE HAS? VERY WELL.

THE TIME HAS COME FOR US TO DEFEAT CAO CAO.

FEI ZHANG! LEAD THE ARMY TO XIAOPEI! THE REST WILL STAY BEHIND AND DEFEND XUZHOU.

YU GUAN, STAY IN XIAPI AND WAIT FOR MY COMMAND. I WILL CALL YOU IN WHEN THE MOMENT IS RIGHT.
AS YOU WISH.

HMPH...

AND I SWEAR I WILL NOT LOSE XIAPI, NO MATTER WHAT.

OKAY, I GET IT. NOT LIKE I LOST XUZHOU. LET IT GO.

LATER, CAO CAO DECLARED WAR ON BEI LIU AND SET OUT FOR XUZHOU.
YU CHENG
MY LORD!
MY LORD!
JIA GUO'S CONDITION IS GETTING WORSE.

TELL HIM TO REMAIN HERE AND FOCUS ON RECOVERING.
YES, MY LORD.

I CANNOT AFFORD TO LOSE JIA GUO. HE'S TOO IMPORTANT.

MY LORD... ARE YOU SURE IT'S NECESSARY FOR YOU TO PERSONALLY LEAD THE BATTLE AGAINST BEI LIU?

IT IS ABSOLUTELY NECESSARY. HE BIT THE HAND THAT FED HIM, AND NOW HE MUST PAY.
I KNOW, BUT SHAO YUAN--
SHAO YUAN IS A BUMBLING FOOL! HE'S A BIGGER THREAT TO HIMSELF THAN ANYONE ELSE!
AND HIS ADVISORS ARE A BUNCH OF BACKSTABBING COWARDS. THEY CAN'T AGREE ON ANYTHING.
SO THE ALLIANCE BETWEEN BEI LIU AND SHAO YUAN WILL ROT FROM WITHIN.

WHEN IT HAS, I WILL PERSONALLY REMOVE BEI LIU'S HEAD.
THEN THE WORLD WILL KNOW THE PRICE OF BETRAYAL. TO XUZHOU!

Cao Cao raised an army of 200,000 soldiers, divided them into five regiments, and set out to attack Bei Liu.

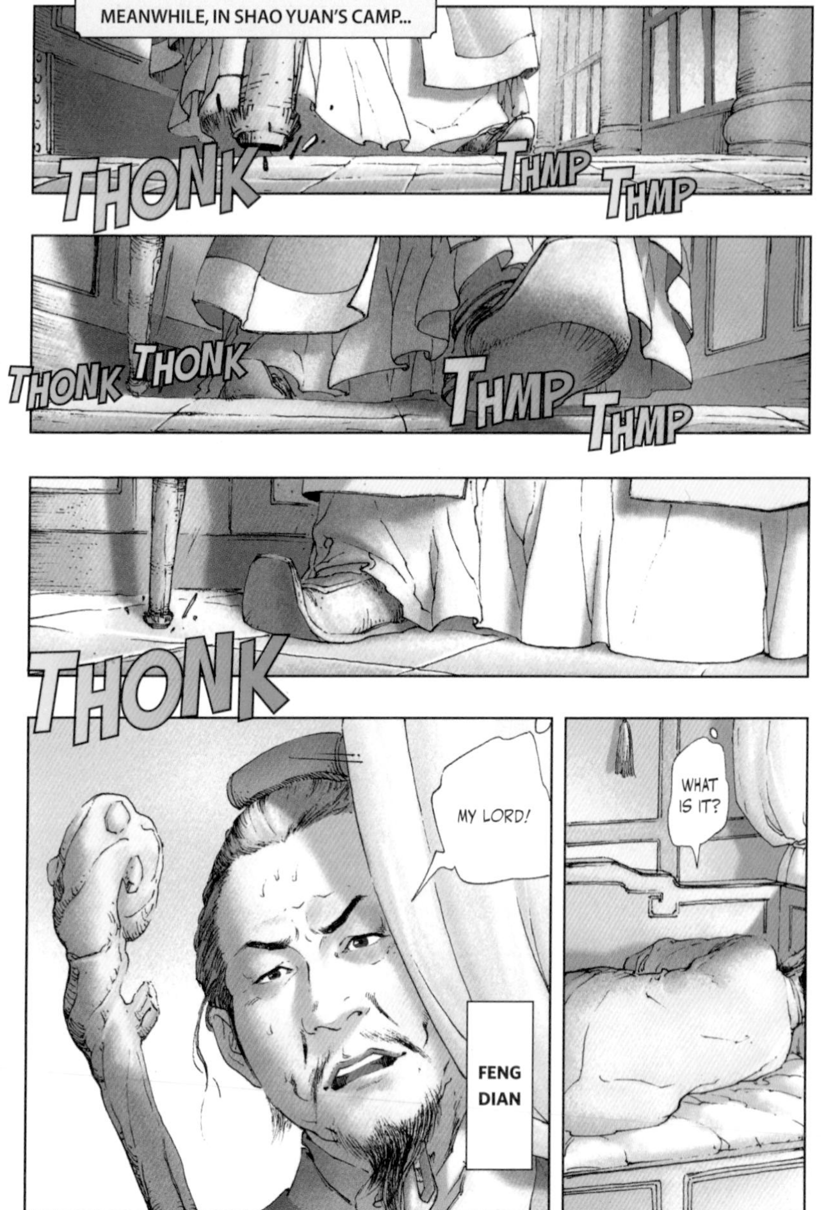
MEANWHILE, IN SHAO YUAN'S CAMP...
THONK
THMP
THMP
THONK
THONK
THMP
THMP
THONK
MY LORD!
FENG DIAN
WHAT IS IT?

MY LORD.
THE ARMY IS READY FOR BATTLE. THEY WAIT ONLY FOR YOUR COMMAND.
MY LORD?
QUIET, FENG DIAN.
MY SON IS VERY SICK AND FIGHTING FOR HIS LIFE.
I CANNOT THINK ABOUT GOING INTO BATTLE RIGHT NOW.

NOW STOP BOTHER-ING ME!
SIGH...
WELL? LEAVE!

MY LORD, YOU'LL NEVER GET ANOTHER CHANCE LIKE THIS.

I'LL BE THE ONE TO DETERMINE THAT. NOW GET OUT OF HERE.

I HAVE TO GO CHECK ON MY SON.

SIGH...

HOPELESS... UTTERLY HOPELESS...

MY LORD!

PEI SHEN
JI PANG
WELL PLAYED. PRETENDING TO WORRY ABOUT YOUR SON WOULD HAVE DECEIVED A MYSTIC!

SHUT YOUR MOUTH!
I'M NOT PRETENDING. WE'RE NOT GOING ANYWHERE.

OH. I SEE...
I BEG YOUR PARDON.

THE SILENT HEAVENS

As one of the richest and most epic stories in Eastern literature, a story of loyalty, power, and betrayal that spans generations, The Romance of the Three Kingdoms has been compared to the classic works of Shakespeare. Indeed, this tale of intrigue and the continuous struggle of several people to take control of a kingdom bears more than a small resemblance to Shakespeare's King Lear, in which an elderly king seeks to divide his kingdom among his three daughters, only to discover they are far more ambitious and cunning than he ever imagined they could be. The resulting conflict between the sisters gives shape to a story about the struggle for power similar to the one presented in Three Kingdoms. But even more interesting than their narrative similarities are what each story has to say about the role the gods play in these conflicts. Or, more accurately, the role the gods don't play.

The worlds of both King Lear and Three Kingdoms are ones that appear to have been abandoned by the gods;

or at least the gods refuse to take an active role in the battle for control of the kingdom. This is in contrast to similar stories from Greek and even Arthurian legends, as well as the classic Chinese story The Journey to the West; these stories and myths act as parables, and the lessons drawn from them are often handed down by deities to the central characters in the story. But Three Kingdoms takes place in a world where the will of the heavens is not made clear to the characters, and this is interpreted to be either apathy or absence. Some of the characters believe there are no gods, as when Cao Cao taunts Gong Chen by telling him that the heavens are deserted. At the same time, Emperor Xian, who as supreme ruler of the Dynasty is believed to be descended from the heavens, is one of the weakest characters in the story, and Bei Liu, one of the stories central heroes, has taken a blood oath not to uphold the will of the heavens, but to restore glory to the earthly realm of the Han Dynasty.

So what is the story telling us, to have the gods

absent from the events depicted? Well, if you take the Buddhist principles at the heart of Journey to the West as a reference point, the highest form of power or wealth one can achieve is enlightenment. To achieve enlightenment, one must be willing to cast aside all earthly desire for material possessions. This is the opposite of what the characters in Three Kingdoms strive to achieve: theirs is a pursuit entirely of earthly desires that can only be measured in terms of material possession, be it land, palaces, or even women. In fact, the gap between the moral principles you would find in a parable and the motivations of the characters in Three Kingdoms are so far apart that it's possible the gods aren't absent at all; it's just as likely that they are trying to make themselves heard to people who don't know what to listen for.

Legends from China THREE KINGDOMS

CAO CAO

Cao Cao is the most powerful man in what remains of the Han Dynasty, having seized power, if not the throne, from Emperor Xian and appointed himself prime minister. Cao Cao uses his royal authority to get rid of rivals, such as the recently captured Bu Lu and Gong Chen. Though he shows no mercy to either of those two, Cao Cao pardons one of Bu Lu's lieutenants, Liao Zhang. Cao Cao is recently allied with Bei Liu, and capitalizes on Bei Liu's good standing with the people by treating him with respect and presenting him to the emperor. But when the emperor discovers that Bei Liu is a blood relative, an agitated Cao Cao calls for a royal hunting party, where he embarrasses the emperor by killing a deer with the emperor's bow.

Some time later, Cao Cao invites Bei Liu for a drink and discussion so that he can determine Bei Liu's intentions and potential as an adversary. Before he can be sure, their meeting is interrupted by the news that Shu Yuan and Shao Yuan are about to form an alliance. Cao Cao gives Bei Liu a small army and dispatches him to deal with Shu Yuan.

Later, it is revealed to Cao Cao that several members of his royal court, along with Bei Liu, have pledged in blood to defeat him and restore the emperor to power. Cao Cao convicts them of treason and kills anyone associated with them, then musters an army of 200,000 to attack Bei Liu, who never returned from his mission to defeat Shu Yuan...

Etched in Blood

Created by *WEI DONG CHEN*

Wei Dong Chen, a highly acclaimed and beloved artist, and an influential leader in the "New Chinese Cartoon" trend, is the founder of Creator World in Tianjin, the largest comics studio in China. Recently the Chinese government entrusted him with the role of general manager of the Beijing Book Fair, and his reputation as a pillar of Chinese comics has brought him many students. He has published more than three hundred cartoons, which have been recognized for their strong literary value not only in Korea, but in Europe and Japan as well. Free spirited and energetic, Wei Dong Chen's positivist philosophy is reflected in the wisdom of his work. He is published serially in numerous publications while continuing to conceive projects that explore new dimensions of the form.

Illustrated by *XIAO LONG LIANG*

XiaoLong Liang is considered one of Wei Dong Chen's greatest students. One of the most highly regarded cartoonists in China today, XiaoLong's fantastic technique and expression of Chinese culture have won him the acclaim of cartoon lovers throughout China. His other works include "Outlaws of the Marsh" and "A Story on the Motorbike."

Original Story

***"The Romance of the Three Kingdoms"** by Luo, GuanZhong*

Editing & Designing

Design Hongs, Jonathan Evans, KH Lee, YK Kim,
HJ Lee, JS Kim, Lampin, Qing Shao, Xiao Nan Li, Ke Hu

Original Chinese edition published by Anhui Fine Arts Publishing House.

Three Kingdoms

Many centuries ago, China was made up of several provinces that frequently waged war with one another for regional supremacy. In 221 BC, the Qin Dynasty succeeded in uniting the warring provinces under a single banner, but the unity was short-lived, only lasting fifteen years. After the collapse of the Qin Dynasty, the Han Dynasty was established in 206 BC, and unity was restored. The Han Dynasty would last for hundreds of years, until the Post-Han Era, when the unified nation once again began to unravel. As rebellion and chaos gripped the land, three men came forward to take control of the nation: Bei Liu, Cao Cao, and Ce Sun. The three men each established separate kingdoms, Shu, Wei, and Wu, and for a century they contended for supremacy. This was known as the Age of the Three Kingdoms.

Written more than six hundred years ago, *Three Kingdoms* is one of the oldest and most seminal works in all of Eastern literature. An epic story spanning decades and featuring hundreds of characters, it remains a definitive tale of desperate heroism, political treachery, and the bonds of brotherhood.

Wei Dong Chen and Xiao Long Liang have chosen to draw this adaptation of *Three Kingdoms* in a manner reminiscent of the ancient Chinese printing technique. It is our hope that the historical look of *Three Kingdoms* will amplify the timelessness of its themes, which are just as relevant today as they were thousands of years ago.

Legends
THREE KINGDOMS

Vol.
05